James Hadley Chase and The Murder Room

》》》 This title is part of The Murder Room, our series dedicated to making available out-of-print or hard-to-find titles by classic crime writers.

Crime fiction has always held up a mirror to society. The Victorians were fascinated by sensational murder and the emerging science of detection; now we are obsessed with the forensic detail of violent death. And no other genre has so captivated and enthralled readers.

Vast troves of classic crime writing have for a long time been unavailable to all but the most dedicated frequenters of second-hand bookshops. The advent of digital publishing means that we are now able to bring you the backlists of a huge range of titles by classic and contemporary crime writers, some of which have been out of print for decades.

From the genteel amateur private eyes of the Golden Age and the femmes fatales of pulp fiction, to the morally ambiguous hard-boiled detectives of mid twentieth-century America and their descendants who walk our twenty-first century streets, The Murder Room has it all. **》》》**

The Murder Room
Where Criminal Minds Meet

themurderroom.com

James Hadley Chase (1906–1985)

Born René Brabazon Raymond in London, the son of a British colonel in the Indian Army, James Hadley Chase was educated at King's School in Rochester, Kent, and left home at the age of 18. He initially worked in book sales until, inspired by the rise of gangster culture during the Depression and by reading James M. Cain's *The Postman Always Rings Twice*, he wrote his first novel, *No Orchids for Miss Blandish*. Despite the American setting of many of his novels, Chase (like Peter Cheyney, another hugely successful British noir writer) never lived there, writing with the aid of maps and a slang dictionary. He had phenomenal success with the novel, which continued unabated throughout his entire career, spanning 45 years and nearly 90 novels. His work was published in dozens of languages and over thirty titles were adapted for film. He served in the RAF during World War II, where he also edited the RAF Journal. In 1956 he moved to France with his wife and son; they later moved to Switzerland, where Chase lived until his death in 1985.

By James Hadley Chase
(published in The Murder Room)

A Can of Worms

James Hadley Chase

An Orion book

Copyright © Hervey Raymond 1979

The right of James Hadley Chase to be identified as the author of this work has
been asserted in accordance with the Copyright, Designs and Patents Act 1988.

This edition published by
The Orion Publishing Group Ltd
Orion House
5 Upper St Martin's Lane
London WC2H 9EA

An Hachette UK company
A CIP catalogue record for this book is available from the British Library

ISBN 978 1 4719 0402 8

www.orionbooks.co.uk

CHAPTER ONE

The offices of the *Parnell Detective Agency* were situated on the top floor of the Trueman building on Paradise Avenue. Founded and run by Colonel Victor Parnell, the Agency was head and shoulders above the other agencies on the Atlantic coast.

After leaving the army, Parnell had been smart to start the Agency in Paradise City, the playground of billionaires. The Agency was strictly for the rich, and there were more rich in Paradise City than in any other city in the United States of America.

Parnell was from Texas. He had inherited his father's oil fortune, and had all the capital he needed to set up the Agency in the lush-plush style expected by the citizens of the city. He employed twenty operators, ten typists, an accountant, Charles Edwards, and Glenda Kerry, his personal assistant.

The twenty operators, all ex-cops and ex-M.P.s, worked in pairs. Each pair had an office, and unless there was an emergency, they knew nothing about the work being done by their colleagues. This system prevented leaks to the press. Should there be a leak, and it happened just once, both operators, working on the case, got the gate.

I paired with Chick Barley, who, like me, had served during the Vietnam war as Lieutenant (Military Police) under Parnell. We were both thirty-eight years of age and unmarried. We had been working as a pair for the past three years, and we had earned the reputation of being the best pair of operators under Parnell's direction.

The Agency handled divorce, parents' problems, blackmail, extortion, hotel swindles, wife or husband

1

watching, and pretty near everything, short of murder.

The Agency worked closely with the Paradise City police. Should an operator trip over a criminal case, Parnell would hand the operator's report to Chief of Police Terrell, and we would duck out of the scene. In this way, the Agency didn't tread on any toes. But the Agency reserved the right to protect a client until Parnell was satisfied that the case was police business, and only police business.

On this bright, summer morning, Chick and I were at our desks, temporarily unemployed. We had just buttoned up a kleptomania case, and were waiting for a new assignment.

His feet on his desk, Chick was reading a girlie mag. He was tall and massively built with sandy-coloured hair and a flattened nose of a boxer. From time to time, he would release a long, low whistle, indicating that he had reached a photograph that made him horny.

Across the room, at my desk, I was doing sums on a scratch pad, and was coming to the inevitable conclusion that I would be in the red once again before the end of the month when I got paid. Money never seemed to stay with me. Every week, before pay-day, I had to borrow. When I got paid, I returned what I had borrowed, and was short again. It wasn't that I was badly paid. Parnell's salary scale was much higher than the other agencies. Money just refused to stay with me.

I pushed aside my scratch pad in disgust and regarded Chick hopefully.

"Old timer," I said, using my begging-bowl face, "how are you fixed with the green stuff?"

Chick lowered the magazine and sighed.

"It's about time you kicked this habit, Bart," he said. "What's the matter with you? What do you do with your money?"

"That's a good question. I wish I knew. It comes and it vanishes, and I have damn all to show for it."

"*I* know," he said, looking smug. "I'm a detective,

2

remember? If you stopped taking that expensive chick around, if you gave up living in that expensive apartment, if you made do with a reasonable car instead of that beat-up Maserati that eats gas, if you let up on the booze, if you stopped dressing like a movie actor, then, and only then, would you stop borrowing off me."

"A good point. In fact, good points, old timer." I smiled at him. "So how about a hundred bucks until pay-day?"

"To hear you talk, anyone would imagine I was a god-damn banker. I can manage fifty, and not a dime more." He took out his wallet, eased out a fifty bill and held it up. "Okay?"

"It'll have to be." I left my chair, crossed over to him and snapped up the bill. "Thanks, Chick. I'll let you have it back pay-day . . . boy scout's honour."

"Yeah, until next time. Seriously, Bart, you had better do something about your spending. If the Colonel knew you were in hock every third week of the month, he wouldn't like it."

"Then he should pay me better."

"What good would that do? You'd only spend it and still be in hock."

"You have another good point," I said. "You're stuffed with good points this morning." I wandered over to the big window and looked way down at the sea, glittering in the sun, the miles of sand and palm trees, and the bodies, half concealed by beach umbrellas.

"Brother! How I would like to be down there with those sexy dolls," I said. "We've just finished a job, haven't we? Why doesn't the Colonel give us a day off as a reward for good work done? Why doesn't he?"

"You ask him," Chick said without dragging his eyes from the mag.

I lit a cigarette, and moving behind him, peered over his shoulder. He turned a page, and we both whistled.

"Now that's what I call a bishop's temptation," Chick said. "Wouldn't I like to spend a week on a desert island with this babe."

3

"And it needn't be a desert island."

"How wrong can you be! On a desert island, you don't have to buy her a thing."

The inter-com buzzed. Chick thumbed down the switch.

"The Colonel wants Bart," Glenda Kerry said and clicked off. Glenda never wasted words nor time.

"Here we go," I said. "More work. What's it this time?"

"Some old trout has lost her dog," Chick said indifferently and settled back with his mag.

I went along to Parnell's office, tapped and entered.

Parnell was a giant of a man with a fleshy, suntanned face, small piercing eyes and a mouth like a rat-trap. He looked every inch a tough veteran, and I had to watch myself every time I came before him, not to salute.

He was behind his desk. In the client's chair sat a portly man, balding, his complexion pink and white, his eyebrows shaggy and his eyes hidden behind green sunglasses.

"Bart Anderson," Parnell said, waving to me. "Bart, this is Mr. Mel Palmer."

The fat man struggled out of his chair to shake hands. The top of his balding head just reached my shoulder. I was aware of keen, hard scrutiny behind the green sunglasses.

"Anderson is one of my best operators," Parnell went on as the fat man sank back into his chair. "You can rely on his discretion." He signalled to me to take a chair and as I sat, he went on, "Mr. Palmer is the agent and manager for Mr. Russ Hamel." He paused to give me one of his stoney stares. "Russ Hamel mean anything to you?"

I don't read novels, but I knew of Hamel. Only last week I had taken Bertha to see a movie based on one of his books. I don't know about his books, but the movie stank.

"Sure," I said, putting on my intelligent expression. "Paperback sales must run into millions. I saw a movie of his only last week."

Mel Palmer beamed.

"I would say Mr. Hamel is in the same stable as Robbins and Sheldon."

I switched to my awe-stricken expression, but wiped it when I saw Parnell glaring at me. Then he looked at Palmer.

"Okay for me to brief Anderson? Have you made up your mind you want action, Mr. Palmer?"

Palmer grimaced.

"I don't want action, but Mr. Hamel does. Yes, go ahead."

Parnell turned to me.

"Mr. Hamel has been receiving poison-pen letters about his wife. She is twenty-five and he is forty-eight. He is beginning to think he has made a mistake marrying a woman so young. When he is writing, he needs to be alone. She is left to amuse herself. These letters say she is amusing herself with a younger man. Hamel is in the middle of an important work." He looked at Palmer. "That's correct?"

Palmer rubbed his fat little hands together.

"It's important if you call a movie deal worth ten million dollars, a paperback deal worth a million dollars and, of course, foreign rights. Mr. Hamel has signed all these contracts, and the book is promised to be delivered in four months time."

I strangled a whistle. Eleven million dollars for writing a book! Man! I thought, are you in the wrong racket!

Talking to me, Parnell went on, "These letters have broken Mr. Hamel's concentration."

"He's just stopped writing!" Palmer said, his voice shrill. "I've told him these letters are written by some sick crank and he should ignore them. If the book doesn't make its date-line, the movie people might sue." He waved his hands. "Mr. Hamel says he can't continue to write until he is completely satisfied that there is no truth in this crank's insinuations. He wants his wife watched."

Another dreary wife-watching case, I thought. Hours of sitting in a car with nothing happening for days, then suddenly, something does happen, and if you're lulled by the sun and boredom, you lose her. Wife-watching was my least favourite assignment.

"No problem," Parnell said. "That's what we are here for, Mr. Palmer. I agree with you that Mr. Hamel's wisest move would be to show these letters to his wife, but, you tell me, he is emphatically against this?"

"I'm afraid so. He thinks it would be insulting." Palmer moved irritably. "There it is. He wants her watched, and a weekly report sent to him."

"He doesn't trust his wife?"

"He has had a previous, most unfortunate experience which has made him distrustful." Palmer hesitated, then went on, "Nancy isn't his first wife. Three years ago, he married a woman of Nancy's present age. This woman felt neglected, and in my opinion, rightly so, and Hamel caught her with some young playboy, and there was a divorce."

"Rightly so?" Parnell quizzed.

"When Mr. Hamel is writing, he cuts himself off from any social contact. His working hours are from nine to seven, and during that time, no one is permitted to approach him. He even has his lunch served in his work room. For a young, newly married woman, this routine can be and, of course, with his first wife, was, a disaster."

The telephone bell buzzed on Parnell's desk. Frowning, he answered, said, "Okay, in ten minutes," and hung up. He looked at Palmer. "I suggest you go with Anderson and give him a description of Mrs. Hamel, who her friends are, what she does with herself during the day if that is known." He stood up. "There is nothing to worry about, Mr. Palmer. Please tell Mr. Hamel he will receive our report, delivered by hand, in seven days' time. When Anderson has all the information you can give him, would you be good enough to see Miss Kerry who will explain about our fees and the retainer."

Palmer looked glum.

"I hope this isn't going to be too expensive."

6

Parnell's fleshy face creased into a wintry smile.

"Nothing that Mr. Hamel can't afford. I assure you of that."

I led Palmer down the long corridor and into my office. Chick hurriedly removed his feet from the desk and dropped the girlie mag into a desk drawer.

I introduced Palmer and Chick and they shook hands. As I was thirsting for a drink, I said, "Make yourself at home, Mr. Palmer. Have a Scotch?"

I saw Chick's face brighten, then fall as Palmer said, "No — no, thank you. Scotch I find a little heavy for me at this time of the day. Perhaps a pink gin?"

"Let's have some drinks, huh?" I said to Chick.

While he was fixing two Scotches and a pink gin, I sat Palmer down in the client's chair, then took my place behind my desk.

"I'd like to fill my colleague in," I said. "He and I work together."

Palmer nodded and accepted a double pink gin that Chick thrust at him.

Every office was equipped with a cocktail cabinet, but the operators weren't supposed to drink, except with clients. We got around that problem by buying our own bottles of Scotch, and keeping them in our desk drawers.

I outlined to Chick what Parnell had told me.

"So we watch Mrs. Hamel, and she is not to know she's being watched . . . right?" I looked at Palmer who nodded. I could see by Chick's expression he, like me, was dismayed to be landed with a wife-watching assignment.

"Let me have a description of Mrs. Hamel," I said.

"I can do better than that. I have brought a photograph of her," and opening his brief case, Palmer produced a ten by six glossy which he handed to me.

I regarded the woman in the photograph. Quite a dish, I thought. Darkish hair, big eyes, slender nose and full lips. To judge by the way her breasts pushed against her white shirt, she was nicely stacked. I handed the photo to Chick who scarcely suppressed a whistle.

"How about her daily routine, Mr. Palmer?"

"She rises at nine, leaves the house to play tennis with her close friend, Penny Highbee, who is the wife of Mark Highbee, Mr. Hamel's attorney. She usually lunches at the Country Club, then apparently amuses herself either with the boat or goes fishing or meets other friends. This is what she tells Mr. Hamel." Palmer lifted his fat shoulders. "I have no reason to doubt her, but Mr. Hamel thinks her afternoons should be checked. He doesn't query her playing tennis with Mrs. Highbee. That, he thinks, would be too dangerous to lie about."

"These letters, Mr. Palmer."

"I have them." Again he dipped into his briefcase and produced two blue-tinted envelopes and his business card which he gave me. Then he looked at his watch. "I have another appointment. If there is any further information you need, contact me. Mr. Hamel is not to be disturbed." He started for the door, then paused. "It is understood that this unfortunate affair is strictly confidential."

"That is understood, Mr. Palmer," I said, giving him my boy scout's smile. I conducted him to Glenda's office. "Miss Kerry will explain our terms."

"Yes — yes, of course." He looked glum. "I am quite sure this is all a waste of time and money, but Mr. Hamel is important people. I must get him working again." He stared at me through his green sunglasses. "If you do happen to get an adverse report on Mrs. Hamel — I am sure you won't — then alert me immediately. There is a lot of money involved."

Ten per cent of eleven million dollars was a lot of loot, I thought, as I ushered him into Glenda's office. I was getting the idea that Palmer was worrying more about his commission than about Hamel and his wife.

Glenda was at her desk. Although she wasn't my favourite woman, she was restful on the eyes. Tall, dark and good looking, wearing a dark blue frock with white collar and cuffs, her hair immaculate, she looked what she was: one hundred per cent efficient and a go-getter.

"Mr. Palmer," I said, and leaving Palmer to face Glenda's steely smile, I returned to my office.

Chick was reading one of the poison-pen letters, his feet on his desk. I saw he had replenished his drink so I replenished mine before sitting down.

"Listen to this," he said, and read, " 'While you are writing your trash, your sexy wife is having it off with Waldo Carmichael. A race horse will always beat a cart horse, especially an old cart horse.' " He looked at me as he reached for the second letter. "This one is a real niftie," and read, " 'Carmichael does it a lot better than you do, and Nancy loves it. Sex is for the young: strictly not for the elderly.' " He dropped the letter on his desk. "Both of them signed: Your Non-Fan. I guess if I was his age and got this crap, I could go in a corner and make whimpering noises."

I examined the letters. They were typewritten. I examined the envelopes: mailed in Paradise City. I then picked up Nancy Hamel's photograph and regarded it.

"I know what's going on in that sewer you call your mind," Chick said. "If you were her, married to a guy who works from nine to seven and leaves you high and dry, you would get something on the side."

"Wouldn't you?"

"Yeah. So . . .?"

I looked at my watch. The time was five minutes after midday.

"According to Palmer, she should now be at the Country Club. I've just time to grab a snack, then I'll get over there. I'll stay with her until she goes home. So, suppose you find out who Waldo Carmichael is? Let's get some dope on him."

On our way to the elevator, I looked in on Glenda.

"I start work as soon as I have fed my face," I said. "How about expenses?"

"Reasonable expenses," she told me. "I've done a nice deal with him."

9

"I bet. I could hear him screaming in my office. How much?"

"Ask the Colonel. He'll tell you if he wants you to know," and she went back to her writing.

* * *

All operators of the *Parnell Detective Agency* were members of the Country Club, the Yacht Club, the Casino, and all the night clubs, frequented by the rich.

All the operators carried The Parnell Credit Card which entitled them to free meals, free drinks, you-name-it-you-have-it in all these clubs. It must have cost Parnell a bomb, but it paid off. There was always steely-eyed Charles Edwards, the accountant, to check on any excessive spending. The credit card gave us operators access to the clubs when working.

I was flicking through *Time* magazine in the super-duper lounge of the Country Club, keeping my eye on the restaurant exit when Nancy Hamel appeared. I recognized her from the photograph, but, in the flesh, she made the photograph a very poor imitation.

She was wearing a white Tee shirt and white shorts, and she had a figure that made me prick up my eyes. There were loads of dishes and beauts in Paradise City, but she was exceptional. With her was a woman, some ten years older, short-legged, wide in the beam, blonde, cuddly, if you like the cuddly type . . . I don't. I guessed she was Penny Highbee.

The two women were in animated conversation. They swept by me, and I heard Penny say, "I can't believe it! At her age!" What she couldn't believe remained a mystery. They reached the exit and waved to each other. Penny ran off to a Caddy and Nancy set off towards a steel grey Ferrari.

I managed to reach the office car as the Ferrari took off. I never used my Maser when on a tail job. I would have lost her except for the traffic. She was forced to a crawl and I tucked myself behind a Lincoln and followed her down to the harbour.

She got out of the car and I got out of mine. She then walked along the quay where the cruisers and the yachts were moored. I tagged along behind her. She paused at a seventy-foot motor yacht. She ran up the gang plank and disappeared below.

There was nothing I could do about this, so I waited.

A big, muscular negro appeared and cast off. Moments later the motor yacht edged its way out of the crowded harbour, then roared off into the sun and the sea.

I watched it disappear out of sight.

On a bollard, clutching a can of beer, sat Al Barney.

Now Al Barney was the ears and the eyes of the City's waterfront. If you provided him with beer, he would let loose with his mouth. No beer: no talk.

"Hi, Barney," I said, coming to rest before him. "How about a drink?"

He tossed the can into the sea, hitched up his trousers over his enormous belly and smiled. He looked like an amiable shark seeing dinner coming his way.

"Hi, Mr. Anderson. Sure, a little beer would be fine." He heaved himself to his feet and walked purposely towards the Neptune Tavern. I followed him into the dark bar. It was empty at this time, but Sam, the barkeep, was there. He grinned, flashing his white teeth when he saw Barney and me.

"Hi, Mr. Anderson," he said. "What will it be?"

"All the beer he needs and a coke for me," I said, and followed Barney to a corner table.

"That sounds good, Mr. Anderson," Barney said, settling himself down on a wooden bench. "You need something?"

A beer and a coke arrived.

"Well, you know: work is work. I saw that yacht leave. Curious. Any info?"

Barney drank the beer, slowly and steadily until the glass was empty, then he set the glass down with a bang.

11

Immediately, Sam rushed over with a refill.

"That was Russ Hamel's boat," Barney said, reaching for the beer. "The writer. Sells big, they tell me." He scowled. "Reading books is a waste of time."

"Sure. The girl who went aboard. Was that his wife?"

Barney's tiny eyes surveyed me with suspicion.

"That's her: nice girl. She's a big improvement on the other one. Now that one was a real bitch. The present Mrs. Hamel is nice. She gives me a wave or a good day. There's nothing snob about her." He drank a little, sighed, then went on. "What's your interest?"

"More interested in the big buck," I lied. "Is he the permanent crew?"

"Josh Jones?" Barney grimaced. "A no-good nigger. A born gambler. Always short of money. He'd sell his mother for a dime if anyone wanted his mother which is unlikely. He works for Hamel. He's worked for him for the past two years. He's a good crew-man, but that's about all."

"Does Mrs. Hamel take the boat out often?"

"About four times a week. Gives her something to do. From what I hear, she leads a lonely life."

"How about Hamel? What kind of a guy is he?"

Barney finished his beer and Sam whipped over with another refill.

"A rich snob," Barney said. "Like the rest of them who own boats. Don't see him often. When he does take the boat out, you'd think he owned the whole waterfront: that kind of guy."

I decided I had all the information I could get from Barney without making him curious, so I pushed back my chair.

"Is Jones a local man?" I asked as I stood up.

"Sure. He lives behind the waterfront." Barney peered at me. "Is he in trouble? It wouldn't surprise me. He's been in trouble before with the cops. They suspected him of smuggling, but they never pinned it on him."

"What time does the yacht get back?" I asked, ignoring his question.

"Six: bang on the nose. You can set your watch by it."

"See you, Al." I settled with Sam, then went out into the hot sunshine. I had four hours to wait so I drove back to the office.

I looked in on Glenda.

"The Colonel tied up?"

"Go in. He's free for twenty minutes."

Parnell was reading a fat file when I entered his office.

"A problem, sir," I said, then told him about Nancy going off in the yacht. "No way of following her. She stays somewhere on the yacht for four hours: plenty of time to get into mischief. Her crewman is black. He reacts to money, but I wanted to check with you before I approached him. He could tell me a load of lies for money, and then tip Nancy I've been questioning him."

"Leave him alone," Parnell said. "Our instructions are she is not to know she's being watched. The next time she takes off in the yacht, follow her in a chopper. Get one on stand-by. It'll cost, but Hamel's loaded."

I said I would do that and returned to my office. Chick was out. I called the helicopter taxi service and spoke to Nick Hardy, a good friend of mine. He said there would be no problem, and one of his choppers would stand-by if I gave him an early alert. With time on my hands, I called up Bertha. She was my current sleeping partner. We had been around together for some six months. She liked my money, and I found her willing. There was nothing serious about our association: no wedding bells. She was a great companion and fun to take around. She had a job with a fashion house doing something or other, and lived in a studio apartment in a high-rise, facing the sea.

Some chick told me that Bertha was tied up with a client. I said not to bother, I would call back, then I left the office, paused at the news-stall in the lobby and bought a pack of cigarettes and *Newsweek* and drove down to the waterfront. I parked where I could see Hamel's yacht when it returned and settled down to wait.

As the hands of my watch moved to 18.00, I saw the

yacht approaching the harbour. In a few minutes, Josh Jones had made fast. Nancy came running down the gang plank and onto the quay.

She paused and called, "Tomorrow at the same time, Josh." She waved and went over to where she had left the Ferrari. As she set the car in motion, I started my engine and followed her.

Glenda had told me that Hamel lived on Paradise Largo where only the real rich dwelt. Paradise Largo was an isthmus in the sea-water canal and formed a link between E.I. highway and the A.I.A. highway. The causeway, leading to the Largo, was guarded by armed security men, plus an electronic controlled barrier. No-one — repeat no-one — was allowed on the Largo without first identifying himself and stating his business. There were some forty magnificent houses and villas on the Largo. They were hidden behind twenty foot high flowering hedges and double oak, nail studded gates.

I followed Nancy's car to the causeway, then sure she was going home, I turned off the highway and headed back to the office. I found Chick pouring himself a Scotch, his feet on his desk.

"Me too," I said.

"Use your own bottle." Chick put his bottle back in his desk drawer. "Any action?"

"Routine." I sat behind my desk. "She played tennis, ate, then went off on a swank yacht. The Colonel says I can chase her in a chopper tomorrow. Should be fun. And you?"

Chick pursed his lips.

"I'm getting the idea that Waldo Carmichael might not exist. No one, so far, knows of him."

I hoisted my bottle into sight, regarded it and found I had one small drink left. I poured and tossed the empty bottle into the trash basket.

"Tried the hotels?"

"All the big ones. I'll try the smaller ones tomorrow.

14

I've talked to Ernie and Wally. They don't know him, but they promise to check."

Ernie Bolshaw wrote a breezy gossip column for the *Paradise City Herald*. Wally Simmonds was the City's P.R.O. If anyone would know about Waldo Carmichael, they would.

"Palmer could be right," I said. "These letters might come from some sick crank, trying to make mischief."

"Could be. I've sent the letters to the lab. They might come up with something."

I pulled the telephone towards me and called Nick Hardy. I booked a helicopter for tomorrow afternoon.

The time was 18.45. By now, Bertha should be home. I dialled her number as Chick began clearing his desk.

When Bertha came on the line, I said, "Hi, babe! How about a hamburger and me for company?"

"Is that you, Bart?"

'Well, if it isn't, someone is wearing my suit."

"I can't eat hamburgers. They disagree with me. Let's go to the Seagull. I'm hungry."

"Not the Seagull, honey. Funds are low right now. Next month, we'll go to the Seagull."

"Ask Chick to lend you something," Bertha suggested. She knew I bit Chick's ear from time to time. "I'm starving!"

"I've already asked him. He came up with a mean fifty."

"Then let's go to the Lobster and Crab. We can eat well there for fifty."

"I'm coming over, honey. We can make plans, huh?" and I hung up.

"Are you spending my money on that extortionist of yours?" Chick demanded. "The Seagull! You need your head examined!"

"We only die once," I said. "No Seagull. What are you doing tonight?"

Chick looked smug.

"I'm feeding with Wally. He picks up the tab. I've

conned him I can give him something: business and pleasure. So long, sucker," and he took himself off.

I typed my report, stating that I had checked out
Nancy, and tossed the report into my out-tray. Then I
cleared my desk and made for the elevator.

Charles Edwards, who handled the financial end of the
Agency, came out of his office and joined me as we walked
to the elevator. He was short, dark, middle-aged and
tough. He glanced at me from behind his pebble glasses
disapprovingly.

"Just the man!" I said as I thumbed the elevator call
button. "Let's have a fifty, pal. Deduct it off my next pay.
This is an emergency."

"You are always asking for an advance," Edwards said,
moving into the elevator. "The Colonel wouldn't
approve."

"Who's going to tell him? Come on, pal, you wouldn't
want to deprive my old mother from her gin, would you?"

As the elevator descended, Edwards took out his wallet
and produced a fifty bill.

"That comes off your next pay, Anderson. Remember
that."

"Thanks." I snapped up the bill. "I'll do the same for
you in an emergency."

The doors swished open and Edwards, giving me a curt
nod, walked away. I thumbed the button to the basement
garage, got in the Maser, gunned the engine which gave
off a deep-throated roar, then I edged the car into the
thick, home-going traffic.

*　　*　　*

Bertha talked me into taking her to the Seagull. She had
a special talent for talking any sucker her way. I was sure
she would talk her way out of her coffin when the time
came.

As soon as we had settled at the table and I had ordered
very dry martinis, I sat back and regarded her.

She looked good enough to eat. Her flame coloured hair, her big green eyes and ochre tan, plus a body that could and did stop traffic, all added up to a scrumptious, sexy explosion.

To look at her, apart from her glamour, you would have thought she was just a gorgeous, sexy bird-brain. She could put on a bright, interested expression that fooled the guys who were suckers enough to imagine that she was sincerely interested in them, longed to listen to their boasting about their big, successful deals, their prowess at golf or fishing or what-have-you, but she didn't fool me. I had known her long enough to know that Bertha Kinsley was strictly interested only in money and herself.

In spite of this failing, she was gay, gorgeous and sensational between the sheets. I would rather spend money on her than on any other girl I knew. She was strictly value for money even though she came high.

"Don't stare at me like that," she said. "You look as if you're about to drag me under the table and rape me."

"That's a good idea!" I said. "Let's show these creeps what we can do together in a confined space."

"Quiet! I'm hungry!" She began to study the menu like a refugee from a detention centre. "Hmmm! King prawns! Certainly! Then something solid." She flashed her sexy smile at Luigi, the Maitre d' who had approached our table. "What can you suggest for a starving woman, Luigi?"

"Don't listen to her," I said firmly. "We'll have the prawns and steaks."

Luigi glanced at me coldly, then beamed at Bertha.

"I was about to suggest, Miss Kingsley, our spit chicken, stuffed with lobster meat and served in a cream sauce with truffles."

"Yes!" Bertha practically screamed.

Ignoring me, Luigi wrote on his pad, smiled again at Bertha and went away.

"I have exactly fifty bucks," I lied. "If it comes to more, and it will, I'll have to borrow from you, chick."

"Never borrow from a woman," Bertha said. "It's not chivalrous. Wave your credit card. That's what credit cards are all about."

"My credit card is strictly for business."

"So what? We're on business, aren't we?"

The prawns arrived.

While we ate, I asked, "Does the name Waldo Carmichael mean anything to you?"

"So it's business." Bertha smiled at me.

"Could be. Answer the question, honey. Ever heard of the name?"

She shook her head.

"New one on me. Waldo Carmichael? Sexy, huh?"

"Still playing name games. Russ Hamel. Mean anything to you?"

"You kidding? Russ Hamel! I love his books!" Then she gave a double take. "Are you working for him?"

"Never mind the questions. You come up with the answers and eat at my expense. Do you know more about him than that he writes books you love?"

"Well, yes . . . . a little. He's newly married. He lives on Paradise Largo. Now you tell me. Why the questions?"

"Just feed your beautiful face." The prawns were out of this world. "Do you know anything about his wife?"

Bertha continued to stare thoughtfully at me and I knew this was a bad sign.

"His wife? I've seen her around. She's too young for a guy like Hamel. Not my type." She gave me a cunning smile. "If you asked me about his first wife . . ." She let it hang.

"So okay. I ask you about his first wife."

"Gloria Cort." Bertha sniffed. "When Hamel gave her the gate for sleeping around, she reverted to her maiden name. Did I say *maiden*? Remind me to laugh some time. That floosie hasn't been a maiden since she was six years old."

"Never mind past history," I said. "Give."

"She lives with a Mexican who calls himself Alphonso

Diaz. He owns the Alameda bar on the waterfront: strictly for the non-carriage trade."

I knew of the Alameda bar. It was the hang-out for the waterfront riff-raff. There were more fights on a Saturday night in that bar than any of the other bars on the waterfront.

"Gloria does a topless guitar act there." Bertha put on her snooty expression. "Can you imagine? When you think she was once the wife of Russ Hamel! That's the way the cookie crumbles. You have it one day: you lose it the next. And let me tell you I'd rather bed with a goat than with Alphonso Diaz!"

The chicken arrived with a lot of fuss. We ate. It was so good, I ceased to worry about what it was going to cost. After we had finished and had coffee, my mind turned to the night before us.

Bertha was quick to respond.

"Let's go, stallion," she said, patting my hand. "I'm in the mood too."

I called for the check, flinched when I saw the amount and parted with my two fifty bills. By the time I had paid, tipped the waiter, tipped the Maitre d', tipped the door-man who brought the Maser to the entrance, I had thirty dollars to see me through to the end of the week.

As I was driving back to my apartment, Bertha said, "I've been thinking about you, Bart. It's time you changed your job. If you and I are going to continue, you have to find something that pays better than being a shamus."

"That is not an original thought," I said. "I've been thinking along those lines for the past year, but there is nothing I can do that would earn me more than being a shamus."

"Think some more. With your experience in crime, there must be something. I met a fella last week who was rolling in the green. He cons old ladies. They give him sacks of money just to smile at them."

"You should be more careful who you go around with, honey," I said. "Gigolos are strictly not my scene."

19

"How about smuggling? I know a guy who is stuffed with loot, smuggling cigars from Cuba."

"Are you trying to talk me into a jail?"

She shrugged.

"Forget it. I know what I would do in your place."

I steered the car into the basement garage of my high-rise.

"So what would you do in my place?" I asked as I turned off the engine and the lights.

"I'd look around among the rich creeps I worked for, and put a bite on them," Bertha said as she got out of the car.

"Meaning the creeps I work for?"

"Meaning the rich creeps like Russ Hamel you are working for."

I joined her and we walked towards the elevator.

"Did I tell you I was working for Hamel?"

"Skip it, Bart. You didn't tell me, but it's obvious. Let's forget it. You are not using your brains. Few get the chance to work for all these rich creeps as you do. Those few who have your chances wouldn't waste them as you are wasting them. There's big money to be made out of these rich creeps. It just means some thought. Come on, let's get upstairs or my mood will fade on me."

As I followed her into the elevator, I began to think about what she had said. I was still thinking when we rolled into bed, but once her arms and her legs wrapped around me, I stopped thinking.

There is a time and a place for everything.

CHAPTER TWO

South-east of Paradise City, some thirty miles out in the Gulf, there is a chain of small islands extending down to Key West.

Sitting beside Nick Hardy in his helicopter, I looked down on this chain of islands that looked like green blobs in the blue, glittering sea.

Nick had no trouble spotting Hamel's yacht. We were already circling the harbour when the yacht slipped its moorings and headed out to sea.

There were other helicopters up: taking the rich on sight-seeing tours, so I had no worry that Nancy nor Josh Jones would suspect we were shadowing them.

I used Nick's field-glasses. I could see Nancy on the flying bridge. Jones must have been in the wheelhouse. I couldn't see him from my position.

"They're heading for the Keys," I said. "Head back to the harbour and circle. We can't lose them, and I don't want them to catch on we are tailing them."

Nick, bulky with a red, good-natured face, did as I asked.

"That's Mrs. Hamel down there," he said. "What's the idea, Bart?"

"Since when did you start asking questions? Ask the Colonel if you want to know."

He grinned.

"Okay. So I don't want to know."

The yacht was now approaching the Keys. It slowed, turned and began running along the coast-line until it reached Matecombe Key, then it headed towards a group of tiny islands about five miles east.

"What are those islands?" I asked.

21

"Used to be pirate strongholds," Nick told me. He was well versed in the history of Florida. "The pirates used to hide up there and pounce on any passing vessel. Blackbeard is supposed to have had his headquarters there. The islands are uninhabited now."

The yacht slowed and began to edge its way into a wide creek, between two of the islands, half concealed by dense vegetation. Then it disappeared under an umbrella of Spanish moss and grape-vines.

I decided it would be too risky to circle and wait to see if the yacht re-appeared. Nancy or Jones, or both of them, might guess we were showing too much interest, and that was to be avoided.

"Okay, Nick, back to the pad," I said, "and if you don't want the Colonel on your neck, say nothing about this."

He gave me a puzzled stare, then shrugged.

"You're the client." He headed back to the mainland. "All the same, Bart, she's a nice girl."

"How do you know? Have you ever met her?"

"Sure, and Mr. Hamel. I took them to Daytona Beach last month and brought them back. I don't dig Hamel. He's a stuffed shirt, but she's a real charmer: too young to have married him."

"Did they seem to you to be getting along together?"

"I wouldn't know. He sat at the back and never uttered. She sat where you are sitting and chatted all the time."

"About what?"

"She was interested in the chopper: her first trip. She asked all kinds of questions: good questions. She's no fool."

So Nancy was nice and no fool, but even nice girls screw around. I changed the subject. I talked to him about his business and asked how he was doing. We were still talking when he landed. As he walked with me to my car, I said, "Keep this close to your chest, Nick."

"Sure."

We shook hands, and I drove back to the office. Glenda said the Colonel was tied up, and how did I get on?

I was about to tell her of Nancy's visit to the pirate

stronghold, when I heard, inside my head, Bertha's voice saying: *There's big money to be made out of these rich creeps. It just means some thought.*

I shifted fast into a lie.

"I followed her in the chopper. She spent the whole afternoon, fishing. A dead waste of time."

Glenda nodded.

"Could be Hamel is hysterical," I went on. "It happens."

"I'll tell the Colonel."

I returned to my office. Chick was out. I hoisted the Scotch bottle from my desk drawer, poured myself a drink and lit a cigarette.

It just means thought.

So I thought. After a while, I decided I would investigate those islands on my own. Maybe Nancy went there to sun bathe in the nude or even to fish, but she might be meeting Waldo Carmichael and having it off with him. Those islands were discreet. Suppose this was what she was doing? Because I was on the Colonel's payroll, I should report to him I had reason to believe that Nancy was suspect. But suppose I didn't? What was in it for me if I said nothing about her visit to the pirate island?

I poured another drink, and did some more thinking, then I pulled the telephone towards me and dialled Toni Lamberti's number. Toni hired out boats for fishing. I had often rented one of his boats on a day-off when Bertha wanted a breath of sea air. I fixed it with him to have a boat with an outboard motor for 05.00.

"How long will you want it, Mr. Anderson?"

"Until midday."

"For cash, Mr. Anderson, I can give you a discount. Twenty dollars: credit thirty dollars."

"Okay, cash."

"The boat will be ready. Help yourself."

As I hung up, Chick came in.

"What's the action?" he asked as he sat down.

"She fished. No action."

23

"For Pete's sake!"

"Yeah, but I enjoyed the trip. And you?"

"I worked my goddamn feet off. I'm now willing to bet Waldo Carmichael doesn't exist. Even the cops don't know him. I've checked all the hotels and the motels. I've even checked the hospitals: no Waldo Carmichael."

I got to my feet.

"Let's tell the Colonel."

We had to wait ten minutes before Parnell was free, then I reported that so far we had come up with nothing.

"It all points to some crank needling Hamel," I said. "From information, his wife is nice, a charmer and no fool. No one I've talked to has a word against her."

"And this guy Waldo Carmichael is not in the district," Chick added.

Parnell pulled at his nose while he thought.

"We can't leave it like that," he said finally. "It's too soon to call off the operation. You've only been watching for two days. Give it to the end of the week, Bart." He turned to Chick. "No point both of you working on this. Something else has come up you can work on." To me, "You take care of Mrs. Hamel. If she goes off on the yacht again, let her go, but keep on her tail when she's not on the yacht. If, at the end of the week, you have a negative report, I'll talk to Palmer and see what he wants done." He waved me to the door and Chick to a chair.

I returned to my office. With Chick off the case, I would have a free hand. It would take me a couple of hours to reach the islands. No one at the office would know I wasn't tailing Nancy. I could spend the whole morning snooping around the islands, and if I didn't come up with something, I could tag after Nancy in the afternoon.

Then I remembered I had nine more days before payday and I had less than thirty dollars in my wallet. I would have to pay twenty dollars for the hire of the boat! I sat bolt upright in alarm.

I was over-drawn at the bank. I sat back and considered

my bleak, immediate future. Unless I found a sucker good for a loan, I was faced with a drink and food problem. I had never been in such a squeeze. I cursed myself for taking Bertha to the Seagull. Then I told myself it had been a super feed. Regret nothing: there must be a way. I began to consider my various friends who had helped out in the past. After mulling over the names, I was forced to admit there was no hope. My so called friends now crossed the street when they saw me coming.

Bertha?

I brightened. An idea. Sold right, she just might be good for a touch, but she would have to be carefully handled. I had never put the bite on her, but there was always a first time.

By my watch, it was 17.40. Bertha usually left the fashion house around 18.00. If I hurried, I might just catch her. I hurried.

Arriving at the parking bay where she always left her Honda, I saw the car was still there. Lighting a cigarette, I waited. Then minutes later, she came briskly from the building.

"Hi, there, babe," I said, catching hold of her arm. "How's this for a surprise?"

She regarded me suspiciously. I could see she wasn't in her usual gay mood.

"Why aren't you working?" she demanded.

"That's a nice way to greet your bed-fellow. Did anyone tell you you look more gorgeous than you did last night? Did they?"

"You can cut out the baloney," she snapped. "What are you doing here?"

"I felt I had to feast my eyes on you. Come over to my car. I want to talk to you."

"I don't want to sit in your car. Take me somewhere for a drink."

Knowing that Bertha only drank champagne cocktails, I tightened my grip on her arm and steered her towards the Maserati.

25

"This is business, babe. I've been thinking about what you said last night."

"I want a drink! What did I say last night?"

I opened the car door and practically shoved her in, then ran around and got in under the steering wheel.

"You came up with a profound idea," I said. "Have a cigarette."

She took one grudgingly and I lit it, then lit one for myself.

"I don't remember what I said. What was it?"

"I'll quote you. You said: 'I'd look around among the rich creeps I work for and put the bite on them.' Remember?"

She lost her sulky look and her eyes narrowed.

"Yes, I said that. So what?"

"I've been thinking. The more I thought the brighter the suggestion became. I have an idea at the back of my mind that I could lay my hands on a big slice of money, and if I do, I won't forget my bed-fellow."

"I hear you. There's a catch in this, but I'll listen."

"I need a very small amount of capital to get this idea on its feet," I said. "How would you like to be my partner?"

Her eyes snapped.

"Are you asking me for money?"

"Put like that, the answer is yes. Strictly a loan, plus twenty per cent interest for ten days. That also buys you a piece of the action."

"What action . . ."

"That must remain a secret, babe." I gave her my mysterious smile. "I guarantee repayment in ten days. You know I wouldn't welch on you, don't you?"

"No, I don't!" She studied me. "Are you going to try to put the bite on Russ Hamel?"

"Who even mentioned him? I didn't."

"You're working for him. You were asking about him last night. You turned shifty when I asked if you were working for him and that told me you are."

26

I sighed.

"Strictly between the two of us, babe, I am. He thinks his wife is two-timing him and he's hired us to watch her, but for God's sake, keep this under your bra."

"That little ninny?" Bertha said scornfully. "He's crazy! She's not the type to play around. All she's good for is tennis and fishing."

"Yeah, but she just might have been led astray. Now suppose she found some rich creep, younger than Hamel, who worked on her. She's lonely, with Hamel working all day, so this creep takes her around, works on her, and finally they have a big romance. It's happened before, and will happen again."

Bertha shrugged.

"Maybe. So where do you come in?"

"I'm working on that, babe. What I need is a little capital."

"How much?"

I could see she was interested. I was going to put the bite on for fifty dollars, but decided not to stint myself.

"Let's say three hundred, and . . ."

"Three hundred!" she practically screamed. "You need your head examined."

"Okay, forget it, babe. I'll find someone else. This is a loan, not a gift. I know dozens of guys and dolls who'll loan me a lousy three hundred at twenty per cent for ten days."

"You are a liar. No one except me would loan you five dollars. Okay, Bart." She opened her bag and took out her purse. "A hundred and fifty, repaid in ten days at twenty per cent."

I peered into her purse. It seemed stuffed with the green.

"Have you been robbing a bank?"

She thrust the two bills at me and snapped her purse shut.

"If you do get your hands on a big slice of money, I expect a rake-off. Understood?"

27

"You'll get it when I get it." I put the two bills in my wallet, feeling rich again.

"Now we'll have a drink. Come on, drive me to Caesar's. I'm thirsty."

I hesitated. A champagne cocktail at Caesar's bar cost ten dollars. I didn't hesitate for more than a couple of seconds. I was rich again. What's money for except to spend?

I started the engine and headed for Caesar's bar.

* * *

I arrived at the pirates' islands a little after 06.30. It had been a hell of a struggle to get myself awake by 04.30, but with the aid of an alarm clock and three cups of strong coffee, I more or less made it.

As Bertha had had a date, after drinking two champagne cocktails, and asking more questions which didn't get her anywhere, she had left me. I had returned to my apartment and made preparations for the morning. I dug out my jungle uniform I practically lived in when in Vietnam. The camouflage blouse, the tuck-in drill trousers, the jungle boots, plus a hunting knife, I packed in a hold-all. I added a floppy hat, insect repellent and a thermos of iced Scotch and water.

On my way down to the quay, I bought a pack of beef sandwiches from an all-night café. I found the boat waiting for me.

When I was in sight of the islands, I cut the outboard engine and changed into the jungle uniform. It felt odd to be wearing those clothes again, but from the look of the dense vegetation of the islands, they were the clothes to wear.

After smearing my face and arms with the insect repellent, knowing the mosquitoes were man-eaters, I headed for the wide creek where Nancy's yacht had disappeared.

I took it slowly: the outboard engine just ticking over and almost soundless. I steered the boat under the canopy of Spanish moss and vines. After the dazzle of the sun, it was as if I was moving into a hot, steamy tunnel. Swarms of mosquitoes buzzed around my head, but the repellent kept them at bay. Ahead of me, I saw the sunlight, and in a few moments, I edged the boat into a tiny lagoon. I cut the engine and let the boat drift to the near bank. I saw a well worn path leading into the jungle. There was a stout post, driven into the bank, and I guessed this was used to moor the yacht. I made my boat fast to the post, then slinging the hold-all over my shoulder, I set off cautiously along the path, my eyes alert for snakes, my hunting knife in my hand. I walked for about a quarter of a mile. Ivory billed woodpeckers and blue jays scattered into the overhead foliage at my approach. The heat was oppressive and sweat ran off me. Ahead of me, I saw the path took a sharp turn, and from the increased light, I guessed, around the corner, was a clearing.

All my jungle training came back to me. I crept forward, avoiding the creepers, making no sound until I reached the massive trunk of a dead tree. From behind its shelter, I was able to see the clearing.

Pitched in the shade was a green canvas jungle tent. It was the kind of tent I used to live in in Vietnam: big enough to accommodate four men comfortably. The entrance to the tent was laced up. To the side of the tent was a portable Bar-B-Cue and two canvas folding chairs. The grass and weeds around the site were trampled flat.

This scene puzzled me. Surely, I wondered, this couldn't be a love-nest? I found it hard to believe that Nancy came here to meet a lover. It must be like an oven inside that tent.

I remained, still, wondering if anyone was inside the tent. The fact that the entrance was laced shut suggested no one was. I looked around, chose a big flowering shrub some yards from the path and moving silently, I squatted down behind the shrub, out of sight, but with a good view of the tent.

Mosquitoes buzzed around me. Apart from bird noises,

the jungle was silent. I wiped my face, opened the hold-all and took a drink from the thermos. I wanted a cigarette, but decided that the smoke might give me away. I settled down to wait. It was a long, sweltering wait. I kept looking at my watch. When the hands crawled to 08.45, I heard a sound that made me flatten out on the ground: the sound of a man, whistling. Then came the sound of the crackling of dead leaves and the swish of vines as they were impatiently pushed aside. Whoever was approaching was confident of being alone. He was taking no precautions.

Peering through the leaves of the shrub, I saw a man come out of the jungle on the far side of the clearing. He was of medium height, broad shouldered and muscular. At a guess he was around twenty-five or six years of age. His black hair was long and unkempt. His bushy beard concealed most of his features. He was wearing a long-sleeved dark green shirt and black trousers, tucked into Mexican boots. In one hand he carried a fishing rod, and in the other, two fair sized Black Crappie, already gutted and cleaned.

As he set about igniting the Bar-B-Cue, I lay motionless, puzzled. Could this tough looking hippy be Waldo Carmichael? I thought not, but it was just possible that he was. Watching his deft movements, seeing the muscles rippling under his sweat-soaked shirt, I thought it was possible a girl like Nancy might fall for him.

With the fish sizzling on the grill, he unlaced the entrance to the tent and went inside. He returned into the open after a few minutes, carrying a tin plate and a knife and fork. I watched him eat. When he had finished the meal and was burying the debris, I decided to take action. Moving silently, I made a wide sweep and got back on the path again. I started off towards the clearing, deliberately making a noise, by scuffling up dead leaves, and as I reached the corner of the path, leading to the clearing, I began to whistle. I wanted to warn him of my approach. I had an instinctive feeling that it would be bad tactics to sneak up on him.

As I moved into the clearing, I saw him standing by the tent. He was holding a .22 rifle, and it was pointing in my direction.

I stopped short and gave him my friendly smile.

"Hi, there! Excuse me. I didn't mean to startle you. I thought I had this island to myself."

He lowered the barrel of the rifle so that it pointed now at my feet, but I could see he was tense and jumpy.

"Who are you?" His voice was low and husky.

I could see I had given him a hell of a scare.

"Bart Anderson. All right for me to approach? That rifle looks kind of unfriendly." I smiled again. "It might go off."

He remained as watchful as a cornered cat.

"Stay where you are. What are you doing here?"

"I'm looking for Blackbeard's cave," I said. "Would you know where it is?"

"There's no cave on this island. Beat it!"

"Are you sure? There was a guy at the Neptune bar who told me for sure it's here."

"I said beat it!"

"Are you a hermit or something?" Still smiling, I began to edge forward.

The rifle came up.

"Beat it! I'm not telling you again!" The threat in his voice was unmistakable.

"Oh, come on. Don't be like that. Don't you want . . ."

The gun went of with a cracking sound. The slug churned up the leaves at my feet. It was a one-shot gun. I moved fast. I was on him while he was groping for another slug.

His reflexes were snake-like. If I hadn't been trained in jungle fighting, he would have crippled me with the kick he aimed at my groin. The kick, a solid one, landed on my thigh and sent me staggering. He swung the rifle and the butt just missed my face. As he swung again, I weaved into him and landed a short arm jab into his belly with all my weight behind it. His breath came out of him with the hiss

31

of a punctured tyre and he went down on his knees. As he was trying to drag air into his empty lungs, I chopped down hard on the back of his neck. He flattened out, face down.

I went quickly to the tent and peered inside. There were two beds, well separated, a canvas wash basin on a collapsible stand and a folding table. On one side of the table were a woman's things: a hairbrush, comb, toothbrush, scent spray and face powder. On the other side of the table were his things: a toothbrush, mug, cigarettes and a cheap lighter.

I looked back at him. He was moving. I went over to the rifle, picked it up, then squatted away from him and waited.

He came slowly alive, pushed himself onto his knees, and then hauled himself upright. His hand massaged the back of his neck as he glared at me.

"Let's be friendly," I said, and stood up. I was watching him closely. There was a dangerous gleam in his slate-grey eyes.

"What are you doing here?" he demanded. "And cut that crap about Blackbeard's cave. What do you want?"

"Let's say I'm looking for some peace and quiet — like you," I said, and smiled at him. "These islands are great if a guy wants to drop out of sight until the climate cools."

His eyes narrowed.

"What are you . . . a deserter?"

"Let's just say I'm looking for peace and quiet," I said. "If you're on the same wagon, then maybe I could confide in you. Are you?"

He hesitated, then shrugged.

"I kicked the Army six months ago. I've had enough of that bull."

I was sure he was lying. He hadn't the stamp of an Army man. After serving three years as an M.P., I knew an ex-Army man when I saw him.

"Well, you have a nice spot here: nice tent. Are you aiming to stay long?"

32

"As long as it suits me. There's no room here for you. Go find another island."

I was thinking about the woman's things I had seen in the tent. Was there a woman on the island with him or were those Nancy's things?

"Okay," I said. "I like company, but if you don't want me around . . ." I shrugged. "I guess I'll look elsewhere. Good luck, soldier," and I walked over to the shrub where I had hidden, and picked up my hold-all.

"How did you get here?" he demanded.

"The same way as you did." I gave him a wave, then started along the path back to my boat.

I hadn't been walking for more than three or four minutes when I heard him following me. He hadn't had jungle training, but he wasn't too bad. If I hadn't been alert, I wouldn't have known he was following me. I kept on until I reached the boat. I knew he was within a few yards of me, but he didn't break cover. He was just making sure I left.

I got in the boat, cast loose, started the outboard engine and headed back down the long, dark tunnel to the sea. I was sure he would watch me out of sight, so I headed back to the mainland, then when the islands disappeared below the horizon, I altered course and made for Matecombe Key. I tied up in the small harbour, crossed the quay to a fisherman's bar.

The negro barkeep regarded me, surprise in his black eyes, then his lips peeled off in a big grin.

"Thought I was back in the Army, boss," he said. "That jungle outfit sure brings back memories."

The bar was empty except for him and myself. I climbed onto a stool.

"Beer."

He uncapped a bottle and poured. I had a thirst that would slay a camel. I drank the beer, pushed the empty glass towards him and lit a cigarette.

"I've been looking at the pirates' islands," I said. "This outfit is right for those jungles."

33

"You can say that again." He poured another beer. "Nothing out there but birds. The Indians used to live there. That was before my time. No one there now."

"Have a beer."

"Too early for me, boss, but thanks."

I looked at my watch. It was a little after eleven.

"Anyway I can hire a rod and tackle?" I asked. "I'm on vacation, getting a little sun."

"I'll let you have mine. I saw you come in. That's one of Toni's boats if I ain't mistaken."

"Right. I hired it for the day. You'll let me have your rod?"

"Sure. I'll get it." He went behind a dirty curtain and I heard him rummaging around. After a while, he came back with a nice little rod and a can of bait.

I put my last fifty-dollar bill on the bar counter.

"Just in case I fall overboard," I said as I took the rod and the bait from him. "I may not be back until five. Okay?"

He shoved the bill back to me.

"We're veterans, boss. I don't need security from you."

I was glad to get the bill back. I thanked him and went back to the boat. When I was out to sea, I cut the engine and changed back into my shirt and slacks. I stowed the uniform in the hold-all, then headed back to the islands. I gave the creek, leading to the hippy's hideout, a wide berth and got under the over-hanging trees of an island some quarter of a mile from the creek. I unpacked the sandwiches and ate them while I thought.

What was this man doing, hiding up on the island? He was no Army deserter. Had he a woman with him or did Nancy use the things I had seen in the tent? Another thing, I told myself: that tent cost money. The hippy didn't look as if he was worth a dime. Was Nancy staking him?

To pass the time, I began to fish, but my heart wasn't in it. I kept thinking and puzzling, but I came up with nothing. I had to get more facts, and more information. All the same, the setup intrigued me.

34

Around 15.00, I heard the distant sound of a motor-boat. I laid down my rod, grabbed hold of the over-hanging branches, and hauled the boat out of sight.

A few minutes later I saw Hamel's yacht approaching fast. It headed for the creek, cut speed, then disappeared under the foliage.

I hesitated. Suppose Nancy had left Josh Jones to keep watch? It would be fatal if he spotted me. So I decided to wait. An hour crawled by. I sat in the boat, slapping at mosquitoes and sweltering. Then I heard the yacht's motor start up, and a moment later, it appeared, and went racing towards the mainland.

I decided to have another talk with the hippy. I could tell him I had run out of gas and could I buy some off him? He wasn't to know that I was sure he hadn't a boat, and Nancy was acting as his life-line. Whether he was her lover or not, I was willing to bet she had got him on the island and probably had bought him the camping outfit.

I started up the engine and steered the boat to the creek. I tied up at the mooring post, then set off briskly down the winding path, making no attempt to conceal my approach.

I reached the sharp bend in the path that would bring me to the clearing. Rounding the bend, I came to an abrupt stop.

The clearing was deserted, and had an empty, used look. There was no tent, no two folding chairs, no Bar-B-Cue. It was obvious my hippy bird had flown, helped by Nancy and Josh Jones. The moment they had arrived, my hippy must have told them of my visit and the decision to pack and get out was a matter of minutes.

At least, it told me something: this hippy was in bad trouble. He wasn't taking a risk that I might tell anyone he was on the island.

I began to wander over the flattened grass where the tent had been pitched. With this hasty exodus, something might have been left behind. After some minutes of searching, I came across the cheap nickel cigarette lighter

I had seen on the folding table. I knelt and regarded it, without touching it. If my luck held, I thought, that flat nickel surface might just carry a fingerprint. I took out my handkerchief, dropped it over the lighter, then scooped it up. I wrapped it carefully, then put it in my pocket. I looked further, but found nothing, so moving fast, I returned to the boat.

The time now was 16.30. I had to stop off at Matecombe Key to return the fishing tackle. I wouldn't be back at the office much before 19.00. It was possible Harry Meadows, in charge of our lab, might still be there.

I started the outboard engine and headed for Matecombe Key.

* * *

Glenda was leaving her office when I arrived.

"The Colonel around?" I asked.

"Missed him by five minutes." She gave me a cool stare. "Anything new?"

"Not a thing. I tailed after her the whole afternoon," I lied. "She behaved as any wife would behave: shop window gazing, tea with a bunch of women, then home. Man! Do I hate wife watching!"

"That's part of your job," Glenda said curtly, and took herself off.

I went along the corridor until I came to the lab. I found Harry Meadows sitting on a stool, peering through a microscope.

Harry was tall, lean and pushing seventy. At one time he was in charge of the Paradise City police laboratory. When it came for him to retire, Parnell had offered him the job of running the Agency's small, but efficient laboratory. Meadows, who couldn't imagine what he would do with himself once retired, jumped at the offer.

"Hi, Harry," I said, shutting the door. "Still working?"

Harry glanced up and nodded.

"Fooling really," he said. "It passes the time, better

than watching T.V. at home. What can I do for you?"

I produced the lighter, still in my handkerchief.

"See if there are any prints on this, will you, Harry, and lift them? I want them checked."

"I'll have it ready for you tomorrow morning, Bart. Do you want the prints sent to Washington?"

"Sure. I want the works on this one." As I was turning to the door, I asked. "Anything on those poison pen letters Chick gave you?"

"They were written on an I.B.M. 82C golf ball machine: delegate type. I got some smudged prints off the letters, but they have been well handled, and the prints amount to nothing. The paper is interesting. I have samples of all notepapers sold in this city. This paper is special. My guess it could be Italian. That's a guess."

Knowing Harry's guesses were pretty accurate, I filed that information away for future reference.

"What happened to the letters?"

"I gave them to Glenda with the report."

"Okay, Harry. Let me know if you find any prints on that lighter. See you," and I went back to my office. Chick had gone. I sat down and did some thinking.

Where had Nancy moved my hippy? I couldn't imagine her bringing him to the harbour which was always crowded. It would cause a lot of gossip if anyone spotted him leaving the yacht. If I were in her place, I would leave him below deck until around 03.00, when the quay was always deserted, and get him off the yacht with every chance of him not being seen.

I decided to spend the night down on the quay. There was plenty of time. I took my .38 police special from my desk drawer, loaded it and put on my holster. Then I left my office, and rode the elevator down to the garage.

It would be dark in another three hours. I wondered if Bertha was free, but decided against calling her. She would land me with an expensive dinner. I warned myself I would have to conserve what money I had.

I drove down to the waterfront, parked the car, then

wandered aimlessly along, past the fish stalls, the fruit vendors, and towards the yacht basin.

I spotted Al Barney sitting on his usual bollard, a beer can in his hand. I gave him a wide berth. Mingling with the tourists and the fishermen, I got by him without him seeing me.

It occurred to me to go to the Alameda bar. I could take a look at Gloria Cort, Hamel's ex-wife, and her boy friend, Alphonso Diaz, and have dinner at the same time.

I slowed as I approached the vast yacht basin. There were about six hundred swank yachts moored to the walk-around harbour. Hamel's yacht was sandwiched between a sail boat and another motor yacht. The gang plank was run in, and Josh Jones sat in a canvas chair, whittling wood with a dangerous looking flick knife. His big body was set before the entrance to the companion way.

I was careful to give him only a glance, then walked on. It looked as if he were mounting guard which pointed to my hippy being below. I was pretty sure there would be no action until after midnight when the quay would thin out, so slightly increasing my stride, I headed for the Alameda bar at the far end of the quay.

This was Wednesday night, and most of the bars were slack. They came alive at the week-ends when the fishermen and the dock workers had money to burn.

As I continued on my way, I saw a news-stall that sold paperbacks and newspapers. I jostled through the crowd. There were several of Russ Hamel's books on display: all of them with sexy, lurid jackets. I bought one: *Love is a Lonely Thing*. The girl on the jacket looked pensive. She had traffic-stopping breasts.

I continued on until I reached the Alameda bar. The entrance was guarded by an anti-fly curtain. Pushing this aside, I walked into a big room with a horse-shoe shaped bar to my left, a dais on which a negro pianist played soft, mournful jazz, and a number of tables scattered around, laid for eating.

There were more than a dozen men up at the bar. Three Mexican waiters, in black, wearing long white aprons, stood around, trying to look busy. The barkeep was a big, fat Mexican who regarded me with an oily smile. He was bald, greasy, and sported a long, drooping moustache. The men at the bar were tough looking fishermen. None of them bothered to look my way. I went over to one of the distant tables and sat down, placing Hamel's book on the table.

One of the waiters, young, dark, came over, and lifted his eyebrows.

"What have you got?" I asked.

"Our special, Signor. Arroz con pollo. Very good."

"What's that mean?"

"Young chicken, rice, red peppers, asparagus tips. Very special."

"Okay, and Scotch on the rocks."

I saw him looking at the girl on the paperback.

"Some chick, huh?" I said.

He gave me a long stare, then walked away. Settling myself on the chair, I lit a cigarette and picked up the book. I learned from the blurb on the back cover that: *this explosive novel, written by the sensational master of American fiction, soon to be a motion picture, has already sold over 5,000,000 copies*.

The fat barkeep came over and put a Scotch on the rocks on the table. He showed me yellow teeth in a friendly smile, then returned to the bar.

After a ten minute wait, I got served. I was hungry, and the chicken looked good. The waiter put the dish before me, nodded and joined the other waiters.

While I was helping myself, three tourists came in: two elderly women and a youth festooned with cameras. They sat down away from me.

I ate. The chicken was tough, and the peppers hot, but I had eaten worse. It was while I was dissecting the drumstick, a woman came from behind a curtain at the far end of the room, paused to look around, then came over to my table.

She had thick hair, dyed the colour of mashed carrots. She had good features, a lush body, showed to advantage by white, skin tight trousers, and a green halter that just kept her breasts under control, but only just. She paused at my table and smiled. Her white teeth were too regular to be her own.

"Enjoying it?" she asked.

I guessed she was Gloria Cort.

I gave her my sexy smile.

"A lot better now you have arrived."

She laughed.

"Lonely?"

I noticed the three tourists were staring with disapproval. I half got up and eased out of the chair.

"Have a drink with me."

She signalled and the waiter came across like a greyhound out of the trap.

"Scotch," she said, and sat down. "You're a stranger here," she went on. "I'm good at remembering faces."

I stared hard at her breasts.

"I would remember if I had seen you before."

Again she laughed.

"I see you're reading one of my ex's books."

I put on a surprised expression.

"Come again. Did you say your husband's book?"

"We parted last year."

"Well, what do you know!" I pushed my plate aside. "Tell me something: what's it like to be married to a best selling author?"

She grimaced.

"I wouldn't know about other authors, but Russ was just a pain in the ass. His books are loaded with sex. Have you read that thing yet?"

"I just bought it. I haven't read his stuff. Knowing he lives here, I thought I'd take a look."

"You think a guy who could write that stuff would be good in bed, wouldn't you?" She leaned forward, her head on one side. "Was I conned? He's as useful to a woman as boiled spaghetti."

"It happens," I said. "Tough on the woman."

"You can say that again."

The waiter came over and cleared the dishes. I said I'd take coffee.

"He's married again, hasn't he?"

"She's welcome. I've seen her: strictly for the birds. There are some girls who don't mind." She gave me a long, sexy smile. "I do."

The waiter brought the coffee.

"Do you like it here?" I said. "You do an act, don't you?"

"Only Saturdays when we get busy. It's all right." She got to her feet. "See you around," and with a smile, she walked over to the three tourists who were being served with the special. She had a word with them, then went back behind the curtain.

I lit a cigarette and sipped the coffee. I had a little information. Russ Hamel could be impotent. I thought of Nancy, seeing her in my mind's eye. If she wasn't getting it from Hamel, maybe a tough hippy would find her an easy mark.

I began reading Hamel's book. It started off with a seduction scene that gave me a hard-on. He certainly could produce a vivid scene.

After a couple of chapters, the waiter came over with the check. I paid, tipped him, then wandered out into the darkness. I had still some hours to kill. I wasn't interested in Hamel's heroine. I would have liked to have met her in the flesh, but on paper, she was too remote. I dropped the book into a trash can, then wandered back along the quay, passing Hamel's yacht.

There was light enough for me to see Josh Jones was still sitting on guard. I gave him a quick glance and kept moving. The tourists had returned to their hotels, but fishermen still moved around or stood in groups, talking. I saw Al Barney still sitting hopefully on his bollard. I kept well clear of him. I was now looking for a place where I could watch the Hamel yacht, and not be seen. I had two hours before midnight. A big moon had come up, making the sea glitter and casting the quay into deep shadows. A small café-bar was shutting for the night. A tired looking waiter pulled down the shutters, then he went inside, closing the door. There was a wooden bench, close to the wall of the café, and under a shabby awning. I went over to it and sat down. I could see the Hamel yacht, about a hundred yards from me. I was sure Jones couldn't see me.

I waited. The life of a shamus consists of waiting, and I am good at it. I watched one group of fishermen after another break up. These men would be out to sea at dawn, and they began reluctantly to make for their homes.

Around 23.00, Al Barney tossed his empty beer can into the harbour and getting heavily to his feet, waddled off into the darkness. By now the quay was almost deserted.

A few night-watchmen, guarding the more swank yachts, stood in a group. A cop went by. Two thin cats appeared. One of them came over and sniffed at my trousers' cuff. I gave it a sharp nudge with my foot, and it slid away.

I now concentrated on Hamel's yacht. It was just as well that I did for I suddenly realized that Josh Jones was no longer sitting in his chair.

I got to my feet, alert.

Minutes passed, then I saw three shadowy figures on deck and I heard the gang plank run out. Almost immediately the three figures were on the quay. They paused to look in the direction of the night watchmen who had their backs turned to them, then they started off away from them.

Keeping in the shadows, I moved after them. As they passed under an overhead light, I saw the taller of the three was Jones. The other, by his shock of black hair, would be my hippy. The third member of the party was a woman. She was slightly built, and wearing a scarf over her head. I guessed she was the one who had shared the tent with my hippy on the pirates' island.

They didn't go far. They turned down a narrow alley. Stepping silently from dark doorway to dark doorway, I followed them.

I saw Jones pause, then beckoning to his companions, he disappeared through an archway.

Cautiously, I peered around the arch, and was in time to see Jones open a door and move out of sight, followed by the other two. Remembering Al Barney had told me Josh Jones had a room off the waterfront, I guessed Jones had reached home.

I moved into the shadows and waited.

A light went on in a third floor window. I saw Jones come to the window and look out, then he moved out of sight.

I waited.

After an hour, the light went out.

Still I waited.

Nothing happened, then as dawn began to lift the shadows, I gave up and went home.

CHAPTER THREE

Some fifteen years ago, Pete Lewinski was considered to be the best and nicest cop on the waterfront. He had patrolled the waterfront from his rookie days, and even the drug-pushers, the smugglers and the young drop-outs agreed they always got a square deal from Pete.

Then one day, Pete bought his wife Carrie, a dishwasher. Everyone on the waterfront knew Pete adored his wife. She was a fat, jolly Swede who liked her liquor, and she, in turn, thought everything of Pete. So, on her forty-second birthday, Pete bought her this dishwasher. Carrie was a good cook, but the clearing up depressed her. The dishwasher was the nicest present, she told everyone on the waterfront, she had ever had, and the fishermen, their wives, the riff-raff, the fruit and shell-fish vendors, and even the drug-pushers, were pleased for her.

It wasn't clear what happened, but three years after the dishwasher had been installed, Pete, returning from a spell of duty, found Carrie dead, beside the machine. It was thought something had gone wrong with the machine and Carrie, with a load on, had fiddled and got electrocuted.

From that dreadful moment when Pete walked into the small kitchen and found Carrie, like a stranded whale, lying on the floor, he went to pieces. His many waterfront friends, worried by his dazed expression, insisted that he should take a little of the hard stuff to bolster up his morale. Pete had always been a mild drinker, and never took a drink when on duty. Finding Scotch blurred the edges of his grief, he began to drink heavily. Chief of Police Terrell who doted on his own wife, was

44

understanding. He talked to Pete, but he could have saved his breath.

Two vicious kids attempted to hold up one of the many waterfront bars. Pete, loaded, appeared on the scene and shot the kids to death. When he was sober enough to realize what he had done, he had wept. Chief of Police Terrell had no alternative but to retire him. The City's administration officer refused Pete a pension. After spending his small savings, Pete became just another of the many riff-raff that haunt the waterfront, picking up a job here and there, living rough.

Through Al Barney who was a close friend of Pete, I got to know this big hulk of a man with his red-rimmed eyes and his close cropped white hair, and when I ran into him, I slid him a pack of cigarettes, knowing that but for the dishwasher, he would still be keeping law and order on the waterfront.

Around 09.00 the following morning after I had followed Josh Jones and his two companions back to Jones' room, I went in search of Pete.

The sun was beginning to show some authority, and I was feeling jaded, after only a few hours sleep. I walked along the quay. It was too early for Al Barney to be on show. He only came out of his room when the tourists appeared, but I found Pete mending a fisherman's net, sitting on an upturned box.

"Hi, Pete," I said.

He looked up and smiled at me. His raddled face was heavily tanned and his blue eyes were watering.

"Hi, Bart," he said. "You're early."

"I'm working on a job. Can you leave that net and have a coffee?"

He carefully arranged the net, then stood up.

"Sure. There's no hurry. A coffee? Yeah, I could use a coffee."

We walked over to the Neptune bar. I noticed Pete was dragging his feet. He moved slowly, like a sick elephant.

Sam beamed at me as Pete and I settled at a table.

"Morning, Mr. Anderson," he said, coming over and giving the table a polish with a dirty cloth. "What'll it be?"

"Two coffees, a bottle of Scotch, one glass and water," I said, not looking at Pete.

"Right away, Mr. Anderson," and Sam hurried back to the bar.

"Pete, I have a job for you," I said, keeping my voice low. "It pays twenty bucks."

Pete stared at me, his eyes popping.

"You can't mean . . ." He stopped short as Sam put a jug of coffee, the Scotch, mugs and a glass on the table. When he had returned to the bar, Pete went on, "What's the job, Bart? Could I use a twenty!" He was staring at the bottle of Scotch the way a kid looks at ice cream.

"Go ahead," I said. "Take a shot."

"I shouldn't, but maybe just one. It's early."

With a trembling hand, he poured the Scotch into the glass until the glass was full. I looked away, hating to watch the further disintegration of a decent, nice man, but knowing he was hooked, and there was nothing anyone could do about it.

I gave him a few moments, then said, "Do you know anything about Josh Jones?"

Pete wiped his mouth with the back of his hand, drew in a long slow breath.

"Josh Jones? There's no one on the waterfront I don't know. He's a no-good nigger. He works for this rich author, Mr. Hamel. He would sell his mother . . ."

"I know all that," I broke in. "I've talked to Al Barney."

Pete nodded. His hand strayed to the bottle. His hand paused.

"Go ahead, Pete. I know you need it."

"I guess." He poured another shot that would have had me walking across the ceiling.

"Pete! I want you to fix it that Jones is tailed. I want to know everything he is doing. He has two people in his room. I want to know when they leave, where they go: a man and a woman. Can you fix it?"

He poured the Scotch down his throat, sighed, stretched his big frame, then with a steady hand poured coffee for me and for himself.

"No problem, Bart. I have a bunch of kids who'll stick with Jones like glue and these other two."

"Then get it organized." I sipped the coffee, then went on. "It's important these three get no idea they are being watched. The man is medium height, black hair and beard. I didn't get much of a look at the woman, but they are together."

"It pays twenty?"

I looked across at the bar. Sam had his back turned. I slid a twenty to Pete.

"There will be more." I took out my business card. "Call me if the man and the woman move. Okay?"

Pete nodded. He was now a cop. The Scotch had brought him back to the time when he had been a good cop.

"You can rely on me, Bart."

"Take the Scotch with you. This is important to me."

He grinned, showing black, rotten stumps.

"Okay, Bart. No problem."

I left him, paid for the Scotch and the coffees, then went out into the sunshine.

It was the best I could do, I told myself. Not good, but better than nothing.

I walked to where I had left the Maser, got in and drove to the entrance to Paradise Largo. I sat in the car with Bob Dylan on tape to keep me company, and waited for Nancy Hamel to appear.

*   *   *

Chick Barley was fortifying himself with Scotch when I returned to the office.

With the money Bertha had loaned me, I had bought a bottle of Cutty Sark. As I unwrapped the bottle, Chick asked, "Whose ear did you bite?"

I sat at my desk, poured a shot and grinned at him.

"I have friends. What's with it with you?"

He blew out his cheeks.

"Don't even mention it. There are times when I hate this job. The Paradise Self-Service store has trouble. One of the staff is taking them to the cleaners. So I walk around the goddamn store, making threatening gestures. What a job! And you?"

"Nothing. It's a complete waste of time and money."

I had followed Nancy to the club, watched her play tennis with Penny Highbee, watched her lunch on a prawn salad, then followed her down to the waterfront. She didn't use the yacht, but wandered around like someone killing time. She bought some oysters and a lobster, then she drove home: a lonely woman, apparently with nothing to do, but now I knew different. I was hoping she would have gone to Josh Jones' place, but she didn't. There was no sign of Jones either on the yacht or on the waterfront.

Having finished my drink, I went along to Glenda's office. She told me the Colonel was tied up. I gave her the report I had churned out on the typewriter.

"Like I said . . . nothing."

"Well, stay with it," Glenda said. "Something might happen."

"Like the end of the world? Which reminds me, Glenda, I'm due for my vacation."

"When this job's through."

"Yeah. You don't have to tell me," and I returned to my office.

Chick was on his way out.

"You see, pal," he said. "The old grindstone tomorrow, huh?"

"Great dialogue. Stay sober," and when he had gone, I began to clear my desk. I decided I would see Bertha. I checked my wallet to see what I was worth. I had just under a hundred dollars and eight more days to go. Maybe I would find Bertha in a less extravagant mood, but I doubted it.

As I reached for the telephone, the telephone bell beat me to it.

"Yeah? Bart Anderson, Parnell Agency," I said.

"This is Lu Coldwell. I need to see you. It's urgent. Do I come to you or you come to me?"

I became alert. Lu Coldwell was the field agent for the Federal Bureau of Investigation. He had an office in the City, but he was rarely there. There was little of interest for the FBI in Paradise City. His main action was in Miami.

"I've a date, Lu," I said. "How about tomorrow?"

"No way. I said it was urgent."

"Spell it out."

"The prints on that lighter you found that Harry Meadows sent to Washington. Up there, they are flipping. You to me or me to you?"

I didn't hesitate. I knew if Coldwell was spotted here by Glenda, she would want to know why he was calling on me.

"Wait for me, Lu. I'll be over in ten minutes," and I hung up.

Now this one, I told myself, had to be played very carefully. My hippy had been identified. If Washington was flipping, this meant he was important. Again, I could hear Bertha saying, *I'd look around among the rich creeps I work for and put the bite on them.*

Play this one very closely to your chest, Bart, I thought, as I left the office and took the elevator down to the garage.

I found Lu Coldwell waiting for me in his small, shabby office. He was a tall, rangey man of around forty, his hair shot with grey, lantern jawed and tough. There were the odd times when he and I played a round of golf together. I made it my business to keep in with the cops and the FBI.

As we shook hands, I said, "You've ruined a date, but always business before pleasure."

He waved me to a chair and sat behind his desk.

49

"This cigarette lighter . . . where did you find it? Why did you check the prints on it?" He rested his elbows on the desk and cupped his chin in his hands. He didn't look over friendly.

While driving to his office, I had prepared my story. I certainly wasn't going to tell him about the pirates' island nor Nancy.

"What's so important about it?"

"Come on, Bart!" The snap in his voice told me this wasn't the time to fool around with him. "Where did you find the lighter?"

"A couple of nights ago. I was down on the quay. . . ."

"Why?"

"This sounds like an interrogation."

"What were you doing down on the quay?"

"I had finished work and I like the quay. I know people there."

"What are you working on?"

"A job. If you want details ask the Colonel. He'll tell you to go to hell."

"This is serious, Bart," Coldwell said, softening his tone. "Okay, so you were on the quay . . . what time?"

"I got down there about ten o'clock. I shot the breeze with Al Barney, bought him a couple of beers, then I wandered down to the commercial harbour. I watched the ships for a while, then as I was deciding to have one more beer before going home, this character appeared out of the darkness. I was feeding a cigarette into my face and he offered me a light, with the lighter you're worked up about."

"Hold it! Let's take this a step at a time. This character . . ." He pulled a scratch pad towards him and found a pencil. "What did he look like?"

"Medium build, stocky, heavily bearded, dark, thick uncut hair, wearing jeans and a dark T. shirt."

Coldwell wrote this down, then opening a drawer in his desk, he took out a folder. From it, he produced a glossy mug shot and pushed it across the desk.

"That him?"

I studied the photograph. It showed a clean-shaven man of around twenty-five with close cropped black hair, lean features and small vicious eyes. The eyes gave him away. This was my hippy all right.

"Could be." I put on my doubtful expression. "The light was bad, and he was wearing a beard and his hair was long, but . . . yeah, I wouldn't want to swear to it, but could be."

Coldwell took back the photograph, found a felt pen and gave the face a beard and long hair and pushed the photograph back to me.

I had no doubt then that this was my hippy.

"Still wouldn't want to swear to it, but I'm pretty sure this is the guy."

Coldwell sucked in his breath.

"So, go on."

"I wondered who he was," I said. "I meet all kinds on the waterfront, and I hadn't seen him before. He seemed jumpy, and he kept looking around as if he thought he was being watched. He asked me if I knew anything about boats going to the Bahamas. I said I didn't, but Al Barney could tell him, and he was sure to find him in the Neptune tavern. I warned him it would cost him a couple of beers. He muttered something and took off. He headed for the tavern, paused as if changing his mind, and I lost sight of him. On the ground where he had been standing was this lighter. I guess he must have had a hole in his pocket." I gave Coldwell my cocky smile. "Being a smart shamus, I told myself this guy might be on the wanted list. From Nassau, it's no sweat to get to Havana. Right?"

Coldwell nodded.

"So I took the lighter to Harry and asked him to check the prints. You know the rest."

"Havana . . . yeah, it figures," Coldwell said thoughtfully. He reached for the telephone, dialled, then talked to someone about boats leaving for Nassau. He scribbled, said he was obliged and hung up. "The Chrystabelle sailed

51

for Nassau this morning. She's an old tub that does a regular run twice a week to the islands. This guy could have smuggled himself aboard. Nice work, Bart. I'll get his description on the wire. He might be spotted in Nassau. It's a long shot." He paused as he reached for the telephone. "Was he alone?"

"He was when he spoke to me. Should he have been with someone?"

"He's supposed to be travelling with his wife. Look, Bart, I've got to get busy, then I'm going down to the waterfront."

"I'll drive you down. My car's outside. If he didn't get on the boat, he might still be around and I might spot him."

Coldwell nodded and began dialling.

"I'll wait in the car," I said and left him.

Getting into the Maser, I did some quick thinking. *Travelling with his wife.* Was that the explanation of the two beds and the woman's things I had seen in the tent?

Coldwell joined me in five minutes, and I headed for the waterfront.

"Who is this guy, Lu, and what's all the excitement about?" I asked.

"If it is him, his name is Aldo Pofferi: an Italian terrorist. He's wanted for three murders and his wife for two murders. The Italian police say they are the most dangerous of the Red Brigade."

"What's he doing here, for God's sake?"

"Italy got too hot for him. He's over here to raise money for the Brigade. Anyway, that's the story. Could be. He and his wife robbed three banks in Milan. The police alerted us to look out for him. They think he reached New York about a month ago. We have been digging around, but have come up with nothing. These prints you found are our first break."

I pulled up on the waterfront and we both got out. Detective Tom Lepski with Detective Max Jacoby came out of the crowd and joined us. Quickly, Coldwell explained how I had run into Pofferi and had been smart enough to have the fingerprints on the lighter checked.

"You'll make a good shamus yet, Bart," Lepski said with a grin.

I considered him the smartest detective on the force: an opinion he shared with me.

Coldwell showed him and Jacoby Pofferi's photo: the one to which he had added the beard and long hair.

"Bart's seen and talked to him. So suppose he goes with you, Tom, and Max and I work together? He's damned dangerous, so watch it."

"Yeah." Lepski looked at me. "Carrying a gun?"

"Always do."

"If there's any shooting, cover me," Lepski said. "Let's go."

Leaving Coldwell and Max to cover the yacht basin and the vendors' stalls, Lepski and I walked along the quay towards the commercial harbour.

"Let's talk to Al Barney," Lepski said. "That old soak knows everything going on around here."

We found Al Barney, sitting on a bollard, holding an empty beer can. He regarded Lepski with a disapproving stare.

"Hi, Al," Lepski said, coming to rest before Barney.

" 'Evening, Mr. Lepski." Barney's little eyes shifted to me, then back to Lepski.

"We're looking for a guy." Lepski gave a description of Pofferi. "Seen him around?"

I knew this was the wrong approach. The only way to get information from Barney was to take him into the Neptune tavern and buy him unlimited beer.

Barney tossed the empty beer can into the harbour as a hint, but Lepski didn't rise to it.

"Seen anyone like that around?" he repeated in his cop voice.

"Can't say I have," Barney said indifferently. "All these young punks look alike."

"This punk's a killer," Lepski barked.

Barney shifted his eyebrows.

"Is that right?" He heaved himself to his feet. "I'm thirsty."

"When aren't you, you old soak?" Lepski snarled. "Have you seen him or haven't you?"

"Not that I remember, Mr. Lepski," Barney said with dignity, and waddled off towards the Neptune.

Lepski glared after him.

I had been looking towards the yacht basin. I could see Coldwell and Jacoby talking to a group of fishermen. I could also see Josh Jones, sitting on the deck of Hamel's yacht. As Barney was walking away, I saw Jones get to his feet, jump off the yacht and disappear fast into the milling crowd.

"The man to talk to is Pete Lewinski. If he hasn't seen Pofferi, no one has," Lepski said. "He should be around somewhere."

Pete Lewinski!

My heart skipped a beat. In spite of his drunkenness, I knew Pete remained a cop at heart. He wouldn't hold back any information he thought would help the Paradise City police. If he were asked the right questions by Lepski, he would tell him of my interest in Josh Jones and the man and woman Jones had taken to his room the previous night. Then Lepski would turn on me. I had given Pete a description of my hippy and he would tell Lepski. If my hippy was Aldo Pofferi, and I was sure he was, I would be in a jam. I could get charged with concealing a criminal, or even worse, as an accessory after the fact.

"Pete's a lush, Tom," I said. "Let's not waste time with him."

"Maybe he is a lush, but he's an ex-cop. That's good enough for me."

He stopped one of the waterfront's riff-raff: a little old man, wearing a battered yachting cap and tattered, filthy ducks.

"Seen Pete around, Eddie?" Lepski asked.

"Not today, Chief. He's usually around, but I ain't seen him all day."

"Do you know where he lives, Eddie?"

"Crab Yard. Number 26," Eddie said, then hopefully, "Got a smoke to spare, Chief?"

Lepski gave him a cigarette, then nodding, he started off across the waterfront. I followed him, feeling clammy in spite of the heat.

Lepski plunged into the back alleys, dark and evil smelling, with old buildings constructed of wood and tar paper: the slum district of the waterfront. He seemed to know where he was going. I tagged along behind him.

"What a hole to live in," he said.

I didn't say anything. My mouth had turned dry. I kept trying to think of some lie to tell Lepski if Pete told him I had hired him to watch Jones.

"Here we are," Lepski said, arriving at an archway that led to a small courtyard, surrounded by high, battered buildings. Tattered laundry festooned the buildings and were strung across the courtyard. Over-flowing trash cans stood outside the entrances of the buildings, and the smell of decaying fish, stale frying oil, urine and rotting vegetables made me breathe through my mouth.

A group of dirty kids were kicking a ball around. When they saw Lepski, the game stopped and they all disappeared down another alley.

At the far end of the courtyard, Lepski found No 26. I had a feeling we were being watched, but looking around, could see no one.

Lepski peered through the doorway of No 26.

"What a stink!"

I looked over his shoulder into a dimly lit lobby: facing, were stairs. To the right, a passage, going away into complete darkness.

"Now, where does he hang out?" Lepski muttered. He moved forward, then taking a flashlight from his pocket, sent the beam down the passage.

At the far end of the passage was a door that stood ajar.

"Let's try this one," Lepski said, and started forward, then stopped. He directed the beam of the torchlight to the floor.

A red ribbon of blood came from under the door.

A gun jumped into Lepski's hand, and he snapped off the flashlight.

"Cover me," he muttered.

I went down on one knee, drawing my police special.

Lepski reached the door and kicked it wide open, then flattened himself against the wall.

Nothing happened. With his gun pushed forward, he peered around the doorway into the room.

Now the door was open, more light came into the passage.

"Hell!" he exclaimed, and walked into the room. "Stay where you are."

I moved forward so I could see into the room.

Lying on the floor was an Indian boy of around fourteen years of age. He wore dirty white trousers and sandals. His T shirt was bloodstained and blood caked his face. One look at his staring eyes told me he was dead.

"Look here," Lepski said, and swung the beam of his flashlight to a dark corner.

Pete Lewinski, an empty bottle of Scotch clutched in his hand, sat hunched up against the wall. His face was a mess of blood. I could see the hole made by the bullet above the bridge of his thick nose.

"Find a phone and alert headquarters," Lepski snapped. "I'll stay here."

As I left the building and started across the courtyard at a run, I realised with an enormous feeling of relief, that poor old Pete Lewinski wouldn't now tell Lepski a thing.

*　　*　　*

It was just after 22.00 when I unlocked the door of my apartment, turned on the lights, closed and bolted the door, then went over to a lounging chair and sat down. I had brought beef sandwiches back with me, but I didn't feel like eating. I had thinking to do.

Pete had told me he had a bunch of kids who would stay with Jones. It seemed obvious to me that the Indian boy, shot through the head, had been one of Pete's kids. Could be Jones had spotted him, followed him back to Pete's place and shot them both. I wasn't satisfied with this thinking, but it would have to do to get on with. Anyway, this shooting told me as nothing else could that Jones and Pofferi were as dangerous as Coldwell had said they were.

The big question mark in my mind was Nancy Hamel. How did she come to get mixed up with Pofferi? I had no doubt she was helping him.

I stubbed out my cigarette and lit another. I was still puzzling, half an hour later, and still getting nowhere, when my front door bell rang.

I went into the lobby, shot back the bolt and opened the door.

Lu Coldwell advanced into the lobby, as I stood aside.

"Saw your light," he said. "These shootings . . . mean anything to you?"

"Not a thing. Have a drink?"

"Why not?" He walked into my living room and sat down and stretched out his long legs. "There was such a goddamn uproar down there, I gave up asking anyone if they had seen Pofferi. I'll get a couple of my men down there tomorrow when the dust has settled."

"My guess is Pofferi has gone, if he was ever here," I said as I handed him a stiff Scotch.

"I did ask around before half the cops in the City arrived. No one saw him. Maybe I'll get the word from Nassau tomorrow."

"It's my bet that's where he is."

Coldwell drank half the Scotch, sighed, then finished the drink.

"What do you make of this shooting, Bart? I took a look. I'd say it was a professional killing. Two shots: two dead. That's the way Pofferi kills. I'm wondering if there's a tie up. What do you think?"

"More like someone had a grudge against Pete," I said. "He fixed a number of drug-pushers in his time. Could be a pay-off."

"Why the boy?"

I shrugged.

"A witness, huh?"

He pulled at his nose and yawned.

"Well, it's Lepski's problem. Pofferi is my problem."

I needed information the way a junkie needs a fix.

"Tell me about Pofferi's wife? Let me get you another drink."

"No, thanks. I've still work to do. His wife? Yeah, I'm interested in her too. I've wired Washington for a mug shot. I'll let you see it. Getting around the way you do, you might spot her and you still might spot him."

"Have you a file on her?"

"It's almost nothing. She called herself Lucia Lambretti before she married Pofferi. The Italian cops have checked out her name, but it's an alias. She emerged from nowhere about eighteen months ago, and ganged up with Pofferi. The Italian cops caught her when she and Pofferi were trying to rob a bank. He got away. She was held long enough to get her prints and a mug shot, then she escaped. Someone smuggled a gun into her cell and away she went, killing two guards." He looked at his watch. "I'm off. See you," and he left.

There didn't seem much else to do except go to bed. It was now too late to see Bertha. I ate the beef sandwiches, thought about Pete Lewinski and wondered if Josh Jones had shot him.

I liked Pete, and I felt depressed, so I gave myself another drink, then went into my bedroom. The bed looked lonely. I wondered if Bertha would come over and share it with me, but decided it was too late. Still, it might be worth a try. I returned to the living room and was reaching for the telephone when there was a gentle ping on the front door bell.

The time was just after midnight. I walked to the front door, slipped on the chain and opened the door a few inches without showing myself. My highrise had had a couple of muggers causing trouble the previous month, and my neighbour was still in hospital.

"Who is it?" I asked.

"I'm Pete's boy." The soft accent told me he was an Indian.

I pushed the door shut, slipped off the chain and opened up.

A thin boy of around thirteen with a shock of thick black hair, dressed in dirty white drill, slid around me, and into the lobby.

I closed the door and motioned him into the living room. He stared around. His breathing came in quick gasps, and there was sweat on his face.

"What's your name, son?" I asked, and walked over to a chair and sat down.

Still staring around, he began to chew his lower lip, then his black eyes shifted to me.

"Joey. I work for Pete."

"You heard what happened to Pete?"

He nodded, gulped, and his dirty hands turned into fists.

"That was tough," I said. "Sit down."

He hesitated, then sat on the edge of a chair, facing mine.

"Why are you here, Joey?"

"Tom and me are brothers."

"Was Tom the one. . . .?"

He gulped again, then nodded.

"Joey, I'm sorry. I'm really sorry."

His face tightened, and his eyes narrowed.

"That doesn't help," he said, his voice husky. "Being sorry."

"I guess not. Why have you come here, Joey?"

He moistened his lips with the tip of his tongue.

"You paid Pete twenty bucks to have Josh Jones watched, didn't you?"

I began to feel uneasy.

"So?"

"Pete told Tom and me to watch Jones. Pete said you would pay more when we had some info. Pete was square. He said we'd split the twenty three ways."

"Do you know who did the shooting?"

"One of the three. I don't know which one."

"What do you know?"

He leaned forward, his black eyes glittering.

"I know where those two are right now. Tom went to tell Pete. That's when he got killed."

I began to sweat.

"Have you told the cops, Joey?"

"After what they did to my dad, I don't talk to cops." His black eyes turned vicious.

"What happened to your dad, Joey?"

"They put him away for ten years. He has another five years to go."

I began to relax.

"So? Where are those two right now, Joey?"

He studied me for a long moment, then he said, "What's it worth to you, Mr. Anderson?"

I took out my limp wallet and checked its contents without letting Joey see. I thumbed out a $10 bill and held it up.

He shook his head.

"I could get killed like Tom."

"Not if you are careful, Joey."

"I could get killed," he said quietly.

Reluctantly, I added another $10 bill.

"That's it, Joey. I'm short."

He hesitated, then reaching forward, took the two bills.

"They are at the Alameda bar."

I gaped at him.

"That I don't believe."

"This morning at five o'clock, Jones and the other two left Jones' place and went to the Alameda bar," Joey said. "They went in by the back way, and then Jones returned to his place. My brother, Jimbo, is there now, watching."

"You have another brother, Joey?"

"Yes. He worked for Pete too."

"Keep watching. I'll pay you more later. I want to know if they move, and be careful."

He got to his feet, tucked the two bills into his hip pocket, nodded and made for the door.

"Hold it, Joey. Where can I find you?"

"Lobster Court. It's right by Crab Court. No 2. Top floor. My brothers and I have a room."

"How about your mother?"

"She killed herself when they took dad," Joey said, his face wooden. "There's only Jimbo and me now."

"Watch out, Joey," I said.

I saw him to the front door, then walked back to the lounging chair and sat down.

I did some thinking. Pofferi and his wife had been hiding on the pirates' island. Nancy had visited them and had taken them on the yacht back to the harbour. Josh Jones then had taken them to his room, and later to the Alameda bar. Why had he taken them there? It seemed to me that Jones, through Gloria Cort, had done a deal with Diaz to hide these two: a much safer hiding place than keeping them in his (Jones') room. He had gone to Gloria because, as Hamel's ex-wife, she knew him, crewman of the yacht. So far, this made sense, but what didn't make sense was why a nice girl like Nancy should be helping a couple of dangerous terrorists. Had she met them in Rome? That seemed likely. Had they some hold on her?

I stubbed out my cigarette impatiently. So what should I do? I knew what I *ought* to do. I ought to call the police and tell them where Pofferi and his wife were hiding, but if I did that, what was in it for me? Nothing that I could see except trouble. Lepski would want to know how I had found out that the Pofferis were at the Alameda. Even if I dreamed up a convincing lie, I would still be left with nothing. No one was going to give me a reward.

It suddenly occurred to me the time was ripe to talk to Nancy Hamel. Would she be prepared to buy my silence?

I grimaced. This would have to be handled carefully. The last thing I needed was to be charged with blackmail.

Blackmail?

I had dealt with a number of blackmailers since I had joined the Agency. I had been the means of sending them to jail. Up to this moment, I had considered blackmail to be the lowest form of crime.

But was this blackmail? All I was going to do was to have a confidential talk with Nancy Hamel. I would tell her I knew of her connection with Pofferi and I knew where he and his wife were hiding. I would explain that a shamus didn't make much of a living. I would give her my sincere smile. Of course if we could come to some financial arrangement, then I would forget the whole thing and everyone would be happy. It was, of course, up to her to decide.

Was that blackmail?

A business arrangement, yes. Blackmail, no.

I am pretty smart at kidding people, but I am in a class of my own when I begin to kid myself.

CHAPTER FOUR

The following morning, around 09.00, I walked into Glenda's office to find her sorting the mail.

"Hi, there," I said, placing my hands on her desk and leaning over her. "How's the busy bee this sunny day?"

She didn't pause in her reading.

"What do you want? You should be on the job."

"Never off it, gorgeous. Those poison pen letters. I need them. I've an idea I can trace the paper. Harry has given me a clue."

"Help yourself." She waved to a filing cabinet and went on reading.

"Business brisk? Lots of new suckers?" I asked as I found the two letters. Getting no reply, I put the letters in my wallet and breezed out of the office.

Taking the elevator down to the garage, I drove the Maser to the Country Club. I parked, then settled in a lounging chair, with a copy of *Newsweek*, to wait.

I had been up early and had made two reports, plus carbon copies. I now felt ready to have a confidential chat with Nancy Hamel. As I sat in the lounge, I thought about her. I recalled the impression she had made on me, both from her photograph and from seeing her. I was sure as I could be that I would have no trouble with her if I handled her right, and I intended to handle her right.

Around 10.30, she came into the lounge, carrying a tennis racket, and dressed for tennis. She went over to the Club's porter, an ageing black with white, frizzy hair, who beamed at her.

"Has Mrs. Highbee come yet, Johnson?" she asked.

I was near enough to hear her.

"She's down on the courts, Mrs. Hamel."

Nancy smiled, nodded and walked across the lobby, heading for the tennis courts. I watched her go. Her hip movement was nice.

After waiting for some fifteen minutes, I went out onto the terrace and saw her playing with Penny Highbee. Lunch time, I told myself, would be right to talk to her, so I went down to the swimming pool, changed and swam. The pool was crowded with the big, the fat, the slim and the dolly birds.

After an hour, I dried off, changed and wandered back to the tennis courts. Nancy and Penny were still playing.

I found a chair under a sun umbrella and sat down. A waiter slid up. I ordered a Scotch and coke. He brought the drink, I signed, tipped and he went away.

A voice said, "It's Mr. Anderson, I believe?"

I looked up to find Mel Palmer, Hamel's agent, wearing an immaculate off-white tropical suit, standing before me.

I gave him my wide, friendly smile, but I wasn't smiling beneath the surface. He was the last person I needed to see.

"Hi, there, Mr. Palmer." I got to my feet. "Have a drink?"

He lowered his bulk into a chair as a waiter came swiftly to his side. He ordered a pink gin, then sat back, his sun glasses aimed in my direction.

"I see you are working." He looked in the direction of the tennis courts, then back to me.

"Pretty dull work," I said.

The waiter put Palmer's drink on the table and Palmer signed. When the waiter had gone, he took a sip, wiped his lips with a silk handkerchief and smiled at me.

"Dull work? This is, of course, good news. Have you anything to report so far?"

"The subject is giving no cause for worry, sir. I have been watching her for the past four days, and there is nothing to report."

His smile broadened.

"Just as I thought. I have tried to convince Mr. Hamel

64

he is wasting his money, but he has a stubborn nature."

"We have checked on Waldo Carmichael, Mr. Palmer. He does not exist," I said.

Palmer nodded.

"I am not surprised. We are, of course, dealing with a sick crank. I have told Mr. Hamel this again and again, but he refuses to be convinced. It is a very worrying situation."

Worrying for you, Fatso, I thought. You're seeing all that nice commission disappearing into smoke.

"At the end of the week, I will be writing a full report on Mrs. Hamel's activities. This report will show that she is leading a blameless, rather dull, life. If my report doesn't convince Mr. Hamel, then nothing will."

"Excellent." Palmer finished his drink, then got to his feet. "I must run along. I can expect your report then at the end of the week?"

"You can rely on it, sir." I got to my feet and shook his hand. "I assure you there is nothing to worry about."

I watched him bounce across the terrace and move out of sight. Then I looked over at the tennis courts. Nancy and Penny had finished playing and were putting on their sweaters. I waited. Talking together, the two women came towards me.

"Have a drink, Penny?" Nancy said as they were a few yards from me.

"Can't stop, honey. I'm late as it is. See you tomorrow?"

"Yes."

Penny hurried away, and Nancy went over to a distant table and sat down. A waiter reached her, took her order and made for the bar.

This seemed to me to be the right time. I waited until the waiter had brought a Tom Collins which he set on the table, waited until Nancy had signed, and waited until the waiter moved away. Then I walked up to her and gave her my respectful smile.

"Mrs. Hamel. I am Bart Anderson. I have just been

talking to Mel Palmer who is, as you know, your husband's agent."

She leaned back in her chair and regarded me. Her cool, dark eyes showed interest, mixed with surprise.

"You know Mr. Palmer?"

"Sure." I gave her my tentative smile. "You play a fine game of tennis, Mrs. Hamel. I was watching."

"Do you play?"

"Well, not in your class. That backhand of yours really rips them in."

I could see from her slight change of expression, she had lost interest in me. I was sure I wouldn't be invited to sit down, so I sat down. I believe positive action gets the business.

She was startled to find me sitting at her side, but, after a very brief moment, when she had stiffened, she relaxed, but her eyes were cool and her expression unfriendly.

"I've been wanting to talk to you, Mrs. Hamel," I said in my most gentle voice. "I am in a quandary."

As she regarded me, she stiffened.

"I am sorry Mr. . . . Mr. . . ."

"Bart Anderson."

"Mr. Anderson, I don't know you, and I am not interested in any quandary you may be in. I can't imagine why you should want to talk to me. I have no inclination to talk to you."

I pasted on my patient smile. Maybe she wasn't going to be that easy to handle.

"You have a point, Mrs. Hamel. If I hadn't your interests at heart, I would now fold my tent and creep away, but may I suggest you give me a hearing?"

"If you don't leave me immediately, I will call a waiter!" The snap in her voice warned me she meant just what she was saying.

So I had to give it to her the hard way. I took out my business card and placed it on the table so she could read it.

"Your husband has hired me to watch you, Mrs. Hamel."

Man! Did that hit her where she lived! The colour went out of her face, her eyes receded into her face, and she shrivelled. For a long moment, she remained motionless, staring at the card, then I saw a little shiver run through her.

I gave her time. I didn't sit, gloating. I looked away at a dizzy dish who was crossing the terrace to the pool. She was long legged, high breasted and blonde: the kind of babe I like to bed with when my wallet is stuffed with the green. I watched her swing her tail, and I wasn't the only one watching. The fat, old finks with white hair on their chests and knotted veins in their spindly legs were also watching.

When the dish had tail-wagged herself out of sight, I turned to look at Nancy.

She still sat motionless, staring down at my business card.

"To understand the situation," I said, keeping my voice low and gentle, "I think you should read these two letters your husband has received. They are the reason why he has hired me to watch you."

She looked up then. Her eyes were like holes in a white sheet.

I took the two letters from my wallet, took them from their envelopes and placed them on the table.

She picked them up. The blue tinted paper rustled in her trembling fingers. I lit a cigarette and waited. I had all the time in the world. A setup like this should never be hurried. I didn't watch her, but shifted my eyes to an elderly couple who had sat down, four tables away. The woman, nudging sixty, was a dyed blonde. She had crushed her fat into a bikini. The man was dyed black. He had breasts like a woman, and body hair a chimp might envy.

People! I thought. The Oldies! They hang on with grim tenacity. The graveyard is around the corner, but they stay in the ring, feebly punching.

Nancy laid the letters back on the table.

"My husband wrote those letters," she said. "Waldo Carmichael is the name of his leading character in the book he is now writing."

I gaped at her. For a long moment, I sat as still as she was sitting. Then I pulled myself together.

"Mrs. Hamel . . . there must be some mistake."

"There is no mistake. My husband uses this notepaper. I recognize the typing. He wrote these letters."

"But why?"

She looked directly at me.

"He wanted an excuse to hire a detective."

I got back on even keel. *He wanted an excuse to hire a detective*. My brain raced. Could be, but why have his wife watched?

I picked up the letters, folded them and put them back in my wallet, my brain still racing. I was aware she was now watching me. I kept my expression dead-pan.

"There are complications, Mrs. Hamel," I said finally. "As I told you, I am in a quandary. I have been watching you for the past four days. I am supposed to turn in a report, covering your movements at the end of the week."

Still very tense, she looked straight at me.

"What complications?" she asked, her voice husky. "Send in your report. It can contain nothing that would upset my husband," and she made a move to get up.

"Don't go, Mrs. Hamel," I said. "Two days ago, I followed you in your yacht in a chopper to the pirates' islands."

She closed her eyes and her hands turned into fists.

"So you see, Mrs. Hamel, I am in a quandary," I went on, watching her. "I came across Aldo Pofferi, a wanted murderer, on the island. You and your crewman, Jones, got Pofferi and his wife off the island. I even know where they are hiding. If I turned in a report covering these facts, don't you think your husband would be upset?"

She sat still, looking down at her clenched fists. She sat

68

like that for several minutes while I waited. I could afford to give her plenty of time to think what to do. I knew I had her over a barrel. This wasn't the moment to put on pressure. I wanted her to come to the right decision without a nudge from me.

Finally, she said, "Are you sending in this report?"

"That's just it, Mrs. Hamel. That's why I am in a quandary. Look at it from my angle." I paused to give her my friendly-understanding smile. "Mr. Hamel hires me or rather, he hires the Agency I work for. It is going to cost him money. I'm just one of twenty detectives paid by the Agency, and paid badly. Although the Agency regards Mr. Hamel as their client, there is no need for me to regard him as my client. Frankly, Mrs. Hamel, I don't approve of husbands who distrust their wives. Unfortunately for me, because I have to earn a living, I have to do what I am told by my Agency." I paused to put on my worried-depressed expression. "So now, perhaps, you see my quandary."

She looked away from me.

"I think so," she said. "Go on."

"Well, that's really it, Mrs. Hamel. I have two reports: either of them I could give Mr. Hamel. The first one will satisfy him that he has started something he should never have even contemplated."

I took the two reports from my wallet and handed her the first one which stated that I had followed her for four days and had found she was leading a blameless existence. She read it.

"And the other one?"

I gave it to her. It was in detail: the pirates' island, Aldo Pofferi, and who he was. Josh Jones. The Alameda bar.

This time I watched her. As she read, her face became whiter, and her hands were shaking when she put the report down on the table.

"What am I to do, Mrs. Hamel?" I asked. "You must understand that I should give Mr. Hamel this second report. If I don't, I could lose my job, and frankly, I can't afford to lose my job. I would like to be helpful. As I've said, I don't approve of husbands distrusting their wives. But there it is . . . my quandary."

She sat still, again staring down at her hands. I waited, but as she said nothing, I decided to help her.

"Of course, if you hired me to look after your interests, Mrs. Hamel, I would be relieved of my quandary. I would no longer be working for Mr. Hamel. I could be working for you. I would then send in the first report without any problems . . . if I were working for you."

She moved, then looked up from her hands, but not at me.

"I understand," she said. "Would you work for me?"

Nearly home, I told myself. Like any sale, the pay-off hinged on the price. We hadn't got that far, but we were nearing it.

"I would be happy to, Mrs. Hamel." I even surprised myself how sincere I sounded.

"What would your services entail?" She was now looking steadily at me. The cold, contemptuous expression in her eyes slightly dented my ego.

"Well, of course, Mr. Hamel would receive the first, negative report and not the second damaging report," I said. "Then I would, if Mr. Hamel was still not satisfied, give him more negative reports until he was satisfied."

She waited. I waited. I had to hitch my smile into place.

"That's it, Mrs. Hamel," I said finally, because the silence and the way she was looking at me began to nibble at my nerves.

"Naturally, you would expect to be paid to work for me," she said.

Well, here it was: the pay-off.

"This would be a business transaction, Mrs. Hamel. Yes, I would expect to be paid. I have to live. If it ever got out that I had turned in a false report, I would be in trouble." I hitched up the smile. "I have a licence. Frankly, that's about all I do have. To work for you, Mrs. Hamel, would be putting my licence on the line. If I lost

70

that, I would be out in the cold, cold world. That is, no other agency would employ me. So . . . I would be taking a considerable risk if I worked for you."

"What would I have to pay?" Her voice was low and her eyes narrowed. "Although my husband is wealthy, I have very little personal money."

I put my smile to bed and gave her, instead, my cop stare.

"Mrs. Hamel, by associating with Italian terrorists, wanted for at least five murders, you have placed yourself in jeopardy. You should have considered the consequences before you opted to give them sanctuary. Why you did this is not my business. You could be arrested and charged with accessory to murder. By helping you, I could also be charged as an accessory. I am offering my help. The pay-off is one hundred thousand dollars."

She reared back as if I had struck her.

"One hundred thousand dollars!" Her voice quivered. "I couldn't possibly pay such a sum!"

"Those are my terms, Mrs. Hamel. It is up to you to find the money," I said, still giving her my cop stare. "A woman married to a man as rich as Russ Hamel should be able to raise one hundred thousand dollars. Don't tell me your husband hasn't given you expensive presents. Look around: hock something. You have until the end of the week. On Saturday morning, I am sending my report to Mr. Palmer. It is up to you if the report is negative or not. Meet me here this time on Friday with the money. If you are not here, Mr. Palmer gets the second report on Saturday morning." I got to my feet, then paused. "Oh, one other thing, Mrs. Hamel. Don't go running to Pofferi. He is a killer. I'm not scared of him, but I have been in the racket long enough to take precautions. A copy of the second report is with my attorney. If anything happens to me, the cops will get it. I assure you, ten years in jail isn't worth one hundred thousand dollars."

I relaxed my cop stare and gave her my bright smile. She sat motionless, staring at me, like a wax figure.

I left her, feeling pretty sure she would find the money.
One hundred thousand dollars!
Man!

*   *   *

The waterfront was teaming with life. Fishing boats,
loaded with crab and lobster and assorted fish, were
returning to the harbour. Tourists were standing around,
gaping, with their cameras. Al Barney was chatting up an
elderly rubber-necker, hoping for free beer.

I picked my way through the crowd, heading for Crab
Court. As I moved off the waterfront and into a dark alley,
I ran into detective Tom Lepski.

"Hi, Bart!"

I put on the brakes and gave him a smile.

"Hi, Tom! How's the thing?"

He blew out his cheeks.

"Still digging. I keep asking myself who would want to
knock off Pete and a boy of fourteen."

"Like I told Lu. A grudge killing and the boy was
unlucky."

"Could be. What are you doing here?"

"Digging." I began to move around him. "See you,
Tom," and started on my way.

Lepski's hand dropped on my arm.

"Coldwell seems sure Pofferi isn't here, but I still like
him for these shootings, so keep your eyes open."

I jerked my arm loose.

"If I see him you'll be the first to know," and I went on
down the alley. Before turning under the arch that led to
Crab Court, I paused to look back. There was no sign of
Lepski, so I continued on, through another archway into a
courtyard that smelt of decay. Kids were kicking a ball
around. They stopped when they saw me, suspicion in
their dark eyes. I kept on and into another courtyard. As
soon as I moved on, they resumed their game.

There was a weatherbeaten sign that read: *Lobster*

Court. Across the squalid courtyard, I found No 2. I climbed creaking stairs. The building stank. The banister rails were ready to fall apart. Each step of the stairs threatened to give under my weight. I kept climbing. Sounds came to me: a T.V. set in full blast: a woman screaming abuse: a child crying: a dog barking. Finally, I reached the top floor. The roof made the top floor into a narrow attic. Ahead of me was a door. The heat up there was enough to fry an egg. Sweat began to run down my face. I rapped on the door and waited, having trouble in breathing. There was a delay, so I knuckled the door again. It opened.

Joey stared at me. His dark little face lit up with a grin.

"Hi, Joey!" I said. "Man! Is it hot up here!"

He stood aside and I walked into a small room with a sky-light; three beds, a table, three chairs and a battered radio. Although the sky-light was wide open, the heat in the room was like a furnace.

"Any news for me, Joey?" I asked, getting near the open sky-light.

"Jimbo is watching, Mr. Anderson. They are still there."

"Sure?"

He nodded.

"They are still there."

"They could be moving." I took out my depleted wallet and gave him another $10. "Keep close watch, Joey. If they move, I want to know where to."

He nodded as he took the bill.

"Okay, Mr. Anderson. I'll get over there right away and tell Jimbo."

"Watch out, Joey."

He lost his smile and a vicious look came into his eyes.

"Yes, Mr. Anderson. They killed Tommy, but they won't kill Jimbo or me."

"All the same, Joey, watch out."

I left him and walked along the waterfront to where I had parked the Maser. Getting in, I drove along Ocean

73

Promenade. It was time for lunch. I stopped off at a sea food restaurant where I ate from time to time.

The Vietnamese owner welcomed me and took me to a corner table. There were a few tourists, already eating, but it was early. The rush would begin later. I ordered the day's special, lit a cigarette and considered my morning's work.

Well, Bart, baby, I thought, you've certainly laid it on the line.

One hundred thousand dollars!

I began to think what I would do when Nancy Hamel handed over the loot. I felt pretty sure that somehow, she would find the money.

Once she paid up, I would give the Colonel the negative report. He would give it to Palmer who would give it to Hamel who, unless he needed his head examined, would call off the surveillance. The Colonel would send in his account and I would be free to go off on my over-due vacation. With one hundred thousand dollars in my sack, I would take off into the blue and Paradise City would see the last of me. With all that green stuff, I could go where I fancied. I had always wanted to charter a yacht and cruise in style around the Bahamas and the other islands. I decided I would take Bertha along for company.

I ate the special while I continued to dream. Man! Would I have a ball!

Then an unpleasant thought dropped into my mind. Suppose Nancy didn't come up with the money? Suppose she was stupid enough or smart enough to tell me to go screw myself?

What then?

I pushed aside my plate and lit a cigarette. This was a decidedly unpleasant thought, but I have always believed in looking at both sides of the coin. So, suppose Nancy didn't produce the money?

Considering this depressing thought, it then dawned on me that I was in no position to put pressure on her. I was in as big a jam as she was. She was concealing two wanted killers; and, by keeping my mouth shut, so was I! If she either couldn't raise the money or decided to call my bluff, I couldn't threaten her with the cops. She would tell them I had tried to squeeze her for one hundred thousand dollars. Cops were always on the look-out for blackmailing private eyes. No matter how fast I talked, they would take me in and give me the treatment. Their first question would be to ask why I hadn't blown the whistle on Pofferi as soon as I had known where his hide-out was. I knew I couldn't talk myself out of that one.

I began to sweat.

Man! I thought, this is beginning to look rough. Then I forced myself to relax. Take it easy, baby, I said to myself. It's not the end of the road. You can't expect to pick up one hundred thousand dollars without a little sweat. So be optimistic. It's a 60-40 bet she won't realize she is in as big a jam as I am. She could find the money, but if she didn't, if she called my bluff, then that would be that. I would give the Colonel the negative report and that yak of Bertha's about putting the bite on the rich creeps would be yet another pipe dream.

The chartered yacht and Bertha, popping champagne corks while we sailed in the sun, began to look out of focus. Still, on Friday, I might be lucky. Nancy might be waiting to hand over the loot.

I then turned my mind to Russ Hamel and the poison-pen letters. This was a puzzle that nagged me.

I recalled what Nancy had said: *My husband wrote those letters. Waldo Carmichael is the name of his leading character in the book he is now writing.*

She had said that with such conviction, I believed her. So why should a rich, famous author write poison-pen letters to himself?

Nancy's explanation was that he needed an excuse to hire a private detective.

I thought about this. Maybe this was the answer. I had no idea how an author created a plot, but it seemed possible that these poison-pen letters were part of the plot of his

75

new book and he was testing for reactions. In his position as a famous author, he wouldn't want to be bothered to approach an investigating agency, but by writing those letters, he could get his agent, Mel Palmer, to do it. This seemed to me to be a cock-eyed method of obtaining authentic material, but Hamel was rich enough to act on a whim, and this could be the explanation of the letters.

Needing authentic details of how an agency set about wife-watching, he had used his wife as a stooge, *believing she was leading a blameless life*. Unwittingly, he had opened a real can of worms.

*   *   *

For the first time since I had been with the Parnell Agency, I found I had no work to do.

There was no point in going to the Country Club to check on Nancy. Whatever she did now was no concern of mine. I had the afternoon before me, then I would check in at the office, making out I had been on the job with still nothing to report.

I was about to make plans how to spend the afternoon, when I remembered, scattered around this lush City, were nineteen of Parnell's operators, all working for a living. It wouldn't do for one of them to spot me relaxing. Chick and I, being Parnell's top operators, weren't all that popular with the other operators. There was always one who might be tempted to put in the knife.

So, reluctantly, I drove to the Country Club and looked around. There was no sign of Nancy. It was just as well that I made the effort to appear to be working for I saw, sitting on the terrace, Larry Fraser, one of Parnell's dim operators who liked me like you like a hole in the head.

He stared at me blankly as if he didn't know me, and then looked away. I took that as a hint he didn't want to exchange words, so I went down to the swimming pool. He was probably on yet another wife-watching stint.

As soon as I lost sight of him, I walked by the pool,

made sure Nancy wasn't around, then took the back way to my car. At least, Larry, if asked, could say I had been on the job.

I drove down to the waterfront. Leaving the car, I walked along to where Hamel's yacht was berthed, but there was no sign of it.

Spotting Al Barney, sitting on his bollard, I went over to him.

"Too early for a beer, Al?"

He gave me his shark-like smile.

"When is it too early, Mr. Anderson?"

We went together to the Neptune and Sam brought two beers.

"Has Mrs. Hamel gone off in her boat, Al?" I asked as we settled.

He drank deep and long, slapped down the glass, looked at Sam, who rushed over a refill.

"She went off an hour ago," Barney said.

"With Jones?"

He nodded.

"No one else?"

He shook his head, drank and set the glass down gently.

"About Pete," I said. "Lepski didn't get anything out of you, did he?"

Barney scowled.

"There's a stupid, ambitious cop," he said with scorn. "Don't even talk to me about him."

"Any ideas about what happened to Pete?"

"Well, Mr. Anderson, I could make suggestions. I liked Pete. Of course, he drank too much." Barney paused to look virtuous. "The trouble with him was he stuck his nose into other people's business, and talked."

"Whose business, Al?"

Barney's bloated, fat face became expressionless.

"There's not much that goes on around here, Mr. Anderson, that I don't know about, but I know when to flap with my mouth and when to keep it shut." He finished

77

the beer. I signalled to Sam who came over with yet another refill.

Barney smiled, nodded his thanks to me, then lowering his voice, he said, "Between you and me, Mr. Anderson, Pete got too interested in Alphonso Diaz, and let me tell you, Diaz is a very tough hombre."

"What interest, Al?"

Barney's face again became expressionless.

"I wouldn't know."

I had gone through this routine with Barney a number of times in the past. Beer produced information, but food unlocked the gates.

"You look hungry, Al," I said. "How about a hamburger?"

Barney beamed.

"Yeah. A hamburger would sit fine right now," and he gave a signal to Sam.

There was a brief delay, then Sam came over with a mountain of hamburgers, soggy, greasy and covered with raw onion rings. He placed the plate before Barney and handed him a knife.

I waited until Barney had munched through the first hamburger, then tried again.

"I'm interested in Diaz," I said. "Any little tip, Al, will be gratefully received."

"Keep away from him, Mr. Anderson. You are a good friend of mine. I wouldn't like anything to happen to you, so keep well away from him," Barney said, his mouth full.

"Why?"

"That's it, Mr. Anderson. Just keep well away from him." The flat note in his voice told me I'd get no further information from him.

I tried another approach.

"Josh Jones," I said. "Give me something about him, Al."

"You keep away from him too, Mr. Anderson. He's a no-good nigger."

78

"How about some of those chilli sausages you like so much, Al?"

He eyed me.

"You know my weakness, Mr. Anderson," and he signalled to Sam who brought over a plate of small sausages, cooked in chilli sauce. Once I had been dopey enough to try one: it had practically blown the top of my head off.

Smiling, Barney began feeding these lethal objects into his mouth. After he had eaten five of them, his eyes began to water, and he paused to take a long drink of beer.

"You still interested in Jones, Mr. Anderson?" he asked, and thumped his chest with his clenched fist.

"Yes."

He nodded.

"I'll tell you something." He lowered his voice. "He and the first Mrs. Hamel, Gloria Cort, had it off together. That was before she hooked up with Diaz. From what I hear, Jones and she are still pretty close."

"You mean while she was married to Hamel, she and Jones . . ."

"He's the crewman. It happens."

"Yes." I watched him start on the sausages again, then asked, "Do you think the second Mrs. Hamel is fascinated with Jones?"

Barney frowned.

"No, sir. Not that lady . . . she's nice. Nothing like that about her. I would have heard. I keep my ear to the ground."

I looked at my watch. It was nearing 18.00.

"I'll move along, Al. See you."

"Sure thing, Mr. Anderson, and thanks for the food." He put a grimy, fat hand on my sleeve. "Remember what I've said: keep clear of Diaz and Jones."

I went out onto the waterfront. I could see the Hamel yacht coming into the harbour. Nancy was in the bows. Jones was steering the yacht in. I mixed with the crowd and headed with long strides towards the Maser. I didn't want Nancy to see me.

Getting back to the office, I put my head around Gloria's door.

"The Colonel wants you," she said crisply. "Go on in."

"Trouble, baby?" I asked.

"Consult your conscience. Go on in."

"My pal," I said, knocked on Parnell's door and walked in.

Parnell was at his desk, going through a folder.

"The Hamel case," he said. "What's new?"

"Nothing, sir. A complete blank. I talked to Mr. Palmer this morning and told him I had nothing to report. He now wants a full report on my work and he is going to persuade Hamel to drop the investigation."

"You are quite sure Mrs. Hamel hasn't been misbehaving herself and hasn't been associating with other men?" Parnell asked, his steel blue eyes probing.

"As far as I can tell, sir, she has been behaving herself, and has not been associating with other men. I have not been able to follow her this afternoon when she took off in the yacht, but when I did in the chopper, she just fished. I am satisfied that Hamel is getting crank letters to upset his work, and that's all there is to it."

Parnell nodded.

"Let me have your report, and I'll send it to Palmer. Gloria tells me you are due for your vacation."

"Yes, sir."

"Okay. Start tomorrow. Have a good time."

"Thank you, sir."

I returned to my office, copied out the first report I had shown Nancy, took the second, damaging report from my wallet and tore it into small pieces.

I went along to Gloria's office and handed over the report.

"I start my vacation as from now, baby," I said. "If you tell me to have a good time, I'll burst into tears."

"Come the day," Gloria said as she began to read my report.

I left her and went along to Edward's office. There I collected my month's salary, plus vacation money. I was rich again!

Back in my office, I found Chick waiting. As soon as I entered, he held out his hand. I returned the $50 he had lent me.

"Where are you going?" he asked as he stowed the bill away.

"I can't afford to go anywhere. I'll chat up the dolly birds and generally relax," I said. "Think of me. If I see you, slogging at work, I'll buy you a drink."

Chick grinned.

"After borrowing the dough from me." He got to his feet. "I guess I'll get home. Have a ball, Bart, but don't spend all your money."

"Just some of it," I said, and sitting down at my desk, I reached into the drawer for the Scotch. "A drink before you go?"

"Gotta date," Chick said. He started for the door, then paused. "I was forgetting. Got something for you. Came in about a couple of hours ago from the FBI." He produced a sealed envelope. "What's Coldwell writing to you about?"

I took the envelope.

"Vacation plans," I said. "He promised to send me the dope on renting a boat."

Chick shrugged.

"Don't get drowned," then he left.

I regarded the envelope, puzzled, then I opened it. There was a brief note and a mug shot of a woman. The note ran: *I promised to let you have this photo of Aldo Pofferi's wife, Lucia Pofferi. Keep an eye out for her. Lu.*

I picked up the mug shot and looked at it. It showed a blonde woman of around twenty-four or five who stared at me from the photograph with hard, vicious eyes.

81

I felt an explosive shock run through me. If this woman hadn't been blonde, I would have sworn she was Nancy Hamel.

With unsteady fingers, I picked up a felt pen and inked the hair black. Again I stared at the mug shot.

I had no doubt now.

This woman, wanted on two murder charges and married to one of the most dangerous Italian terrorists was Nancy Hamel!

CHAPTER FIVE

Fanny Battley, the night clerk in charge of *The Paradise City Herald*'s morgue, looked up as I entered the big room, lined with folios containing the back editions of the newspaper, and steel cabinets containing a complete record of all the photographs that had appeared in the paper since its inception.

The Parnell operators often made use of the facilities of the morgue, and we were all well known to Fanny, a lively coloured girl, good at her job and always helpful.

"Hi, Bart! Don't tell me you're still working?" she said with a wide smile of welcome.

"Hi, Fan!" I came to rest at her desk. "I'm going on vacation tomorrow. I have one little job to clear up."

"Lucky you! Where are you going?"

"Who wants to go anywhere but here? Look, honey, I need a little help. I want to know when and who to and where Russ Hamel, the author, married."

"No problem. Sit down." She waved to a desk. "I'll bring you what we've got."

That was the big thing about Fanny. She never asked questions.

I sat down, lit a cigarette and waited. She went nimbly through a big card index, then crossed over to one of the folios, dragged it out and dumped it on my desk.

"Have you any photographs of the happy pair?" I asked.

She produced an envelope from one of the steel cabinets and put it on the desk.

"That's all we have, Bart."

"Fine, Fan, and thanks."

She went back to her desk and resumed card indexing.

83

I looked at the photographs. Russ Hamel turned out to be a square faced, heavily built man, handsome, with greying hair, and with that arrogant look of a rich man who is sure of his success. I concentrated on Nancy's photographs. In all of them, she wore dark, goggle sunglasses that successfully screened her face. Anyone seeing her on the streets wouldn't have known her by these photographs.

I read through the wedding account. Interviewed, Hamel said he had met Nancy in Rome. There had been a whirlwind courtship, and they had married two months after their first meeting. Hamel said Nancy was too shy to comment, and he didn't want her bothered.

I paused to check dates, and worked out that Hamel had met her eight months ago. I then remembered Coldwell had said she had begun criminal operations with Pofferi eighteen months ago. It occurred to me, with a feeling of shock, that she was married to Pofferi when she had married Hamel! Had she married Hamel to get out of Italy after her arrest and murderous escape? I liked this idea: who would suspect the wife of Russ Hamel to be a wanted terrorist?

Satisfied there was no other information in the article of any use to me, I carried the folio back to its shelf.

"Thanks, Fan." I gave her the envelope containing the photographs. "That about buttons it up. See you around," and blowing her a kiss, I left her.

I sat in the Maser and considered my next move. Tomorrow, at midday, I was to meet Nancy at the Country Club. With my usual optimism, I thought there was still a slim chance of her producing the money, but if she didn't, I was now in a very good position to put on the pressure. To tell her I could now prove she was Lucia Pofferi would surely produce the green.

This new information needed quiet and careful thought. I decided to return home, put my feet up and exercise my brain. I set the car in motion, and on the way, I stopped at a sandwich bar and bought a pack of sandwiches.

As I was turning onto the street, leading to my highrise, a small figure darted out of the shadows, frantically waving.

I stood on the brake pedal and the Maser squealed to a stop.

Joey appeared at my window.

"Don't go home, Mr. Anderson," he said urgently. "They are waiting for you."

Behind me, a car hooted. Joey ran around the Maser, opened the passenger's door and scrambled in beside me. I eased the car to the kerb.

"Gone to sleep, bird-brain?" the driver in the car behind me bawled, and drove on.

"What is it, Joey?" I asked.

"Diaz and Jones," Joey said breathlessly. "I followed them. They went to your place. I saw a light flash on and off in your apartment. They are still there."

I felt a prickly sensation run up my spine. Nancy had blown the whistle on me! She had gone to Diaz and told him I was twisting her arm! I remembered Al Barney's warning to keep clear of Diaz and Jones. I broke out into a cold sweat.

Joey nudged me.

"I'm looking after you, Mr. Anderson," he said.

"You can say that again, Joey. Stay still for a moment. I want to think."

"I'm hungry, Mr. Anderson."

I saw he had found the pack of sandwiches and was fondling it.

"Go ahead," I said. "Just relax with the mouth."

While he was munching, I considered what I was to do. I thought of Pete who had got too close to Diaz and had been ruthlessly wiped out. I remembered I had told Nancy that I had given a statement to my lawyer that would not only incriminate her, but give away Pofferi's hiding place. Maybe Diaz thought I was bluffing and had moved into

85

action. He would be right that I had been bluffing, so now, I had to make the bluff stick. I would have to write a complete statement, including the fact that I knew Nancy was Pofferi's wife. I would then show the statement to Diaz plus a receipt from my lawyer that the original statement was in his hands. In this way, and only this way, would I be able to draw Diaz's teeth.

After further thought, I decided to go to my office and use my typewriter there. I was not, repeat not, returning to my apartment. The agency's nightguard would let me in and I could park the Maser in the underground garage, out of sight.

"Okay, Joey," I said. "You get back and watch. When they leave, call me."

I gave him my business card.

With his mouth full, he nodded, staring hard at me with his bright, little eyes. I took the hint and gave him a $20 bill. He grinned, slid out of the car and was away.

Jackson, the Agency's nightguard, opened the door after I had rung a couple of times.

"Have you forgotten something, Mr. Anderson?" he asked as I stepped around him and into the reception lobby.

"Clearing my desk," I said. "I'm going on vacation tomorrow."

"Have a good time, Mr. Anderson."

I hope so, I thought. Man! I hope so!

It took me close on two hours to get my statement right, and I made three copies. I then went along to the typist pool and ran off three photo-copies of the mug shots of Pofferi and Nancy, Coldwell had given me.

Returning to my office, I pinned the mug shots to the copies of the statement, then put them in separate envelopes. On each envelope, I typed: *To be handed to Chief of Police Terrell in the event of my death or if I go missing.*

I then found a larger envelope and put the envelope containing the top copy of my statement, plus the original mug shots into the larger envelope. I addressed the envelope to Howard Selby, a smart attorney with whom the Agency often did business and who was a good friend of mine. I then wrote him a letter, telling him I was on to a dangerous gang and was collecting evidence against them. I wanted him to keep the enclosed envelope (unopened) until I had completed my case. I had been threatened, so I was taking out insurance by giving him half the evidence. I concluded by saying if he heard of my death or that I had gone missing, he was to give the envelope to Chief of Police Terrell. I wanted a letter from him stating these facts and this letter must reach me at my home address by special messenger before midday tomorrow.

Selby had offices on the fifth floor of the Trueman building. I took the elevator down and put the letter in his mail box, then returned to my office.

The nightguard watched these manoeuvres with a blank stare, but he kept from asking questions.

I sat again behind my desk and managed to grin. At least, I was nearly safe. I put the second envelope between the pages of *Robertson's Law Index* and the book into my Scotch bottle drawer. Seeing there was still some Scotch left, I made myself a drink. The third envelope I put in my wallet.

As I sipped my drink, my thoughts turned once again to owning one hundred thousand dollars. Would Nancy be at the Country Club tomorrow at midday? I rather doubted it. She had gone to Diaz for help. His immediate reaction was to go to my apartment and wait for me. Was he waiting with a gun or waiting to do a deal?

I finished my drink and was considering pouring another when my telephone came alive.

Joey said, "They left five minutes ago, Mr. Anderson, and are heading back to the Alameda."

"Thank's, Joey. Get some sleep. How's Jimbo?"

"He's watching the Alameda, Mr. Anderson."

"Keep watching, Joey. If you have news, call me at my apartment."

"Yes Mr. Anderson," and he rang off.

I now needed some sleep. I said goodnight to the night-guard, went down to the garage and drove home.

Not a bad day's work, I thought, as I let myself into my apartment. Tomorrow would be the crunch.

Looking around, I found nothing had been disturbed. There was some cigar ash on the carpet, but otherwise I wouldn't have known Diaz and Jones had been here.

Tomorrow! I had already decided what I would do. I was very confident. I shot the bolt on the front door and headed for my bedroom.

I could almost hear the rustle of the green stuff: my idea of sweet music.

* * *

I came awake with a start. Someone was ringing on my front door bell. Cursing, I levered myself out of bed and looked blearily at my watch. The time was 10.35.

I called through the door: "Who is it?"

"From Mr. Selby," a girl's voice said.

I opened up and accepted an envelope from one of Selby's clerks. She was the mousey type who expected to be raped at any moment. She gave me a scared stare and retreated.

I opened the envelope and took out the letter:

Dear Bart Anderson,

This acknowledges that I have an envelope from you on which is written: "To be handed to the Chief of Police Terrell in the event of my death or if I go missing."

I have arranged for the envelope's safe keeping, and will follow out your instructions.

Yours etc.

Howard Selby.

Humming under my breath, I put the letter on my desk, then went into the kitchen and made coffee. I felt I had taken out all the insurance I needed.

At 11.30, shaved, showered and wearing my fancy

cream and blue striped suit, I locked up my apartment and went down to the Maser.

I drove to the Country Club, parked and wandered into the spacious lobby. The time now was 11.55. I asked the porter if Mrs. Hamel had arrived.

"No, sir, not yet," he told me.

I sat down where I could see the entrance, lit a cigarette and waited. I wasn't expecting her to show, but I went through the motions. We had a date, but if she didn't keep it, I would shift to operation B.

I waited until 12.30, then I went into the restaurant and had the Club salad, taking my time. Just to make sure, after my lunch, I wandered down to the tennis courts and around the pool. Nancy Hamel was not in evidence.

So, operation B.

Bart, baby, I said to myself, as I walked to the parking lot, you can't expect to pick up one hundred thousand dollars without working for it. So work for it.

I drove down to the waterfront, parked within sight of the Alameda bar, left the car and crossed the crowded waterfront to the Alameda entrance. Pushing aside the bead curtains, I walked into the big room.

There was a number of waterfront riff-raff up at the bar. Several tourists were eating at the tables. The Mexican waiters were busy, serving.

The fat barkeep gave me an oily smile as I walked up to the bar.

"Mr. Diaz," I said. "Where do I find him?"

The barkeep's little eyes widened.

"You want Mr. Diaz?"

"You deaf or something?" I gave him a smile to take the curse off it.

"Mr. Diaz is busy."

"So am I. Hurry it up, fatso. Tell him it's Bart Anderson."

He hesitated, then moved down the bar to a telephone. He spoke softly, nodded and hung up.

"Through there," he said, and pointed to a door at the far end of the room.

I walked over to the door, opened it and stepped into a room furnished as an office: a desk facing me, filing cabinets to the right and left of me, two telephones on the desk and a smaller desk on which stood a typewriter.

Sitting behind the bigger desk was a slim, middle aged man who regarded me with glittering, flat eyes a cobra might envy. His thick, well oiled black hair grew down to his collar. He had a black moustache that climbed down either side of his face to his chin. Looking at him, I saw why Al Barney had warned me about him. As Barney had said, this Mexican was a very tough hombre.

"Mr. Diaz?" I said, closing the door and leaning against it.

He nodded, found a matchstick and began to probe his teeth.

"Are you acting for Lucia Pofferi?" I asked, watching him.

His face remained dead-pan.

"You've got a wrong number," he said.

"Maybe you are acting for Nancy Hamel?"

"Maybe."

"I had a date with her at the Country Club. She didn't show."

He lifted his shoulders and looked bored.

"I was expecting her to hand over a lump of the green," I said. "No green."

Again he lifted his shoulders and looked more bored.

I saw this was going to take a little time. I pulled an upright chair up to his desk and sat astride it. Then I took out the envelope containing a copy of my detailed statement and dropped it in front of him.

He eyed it and read what I had written on it.

"Are you expecting to die?" he asked quietly.

"Well, Pete Lewinski did. No, I'm not expecting to die now."

He lifted his eyebrows.

"Don't bet on it."

"Go ahead and read what's in the envelope. It's for you to keep. After you've read it, maybe you'll stop acting like a fugitive from a B movie, and start talking sense."

His eyes gleamed, but his face remained expressionless. Then he picked up a thin bladed knife lying on his desk, slit open the envelope and extracted the typewritten pages.

I lit a cigarette and watched him. He first examined the mug shots. They might have been blank bits of paper for all the impact they appeared to make on him. Then leaning back in his chair, he read through the five pages of typewriting, his face still expressionless.

I would hate to play poker with him, I thought as I waited.

Finally he laid down the sheets of paper and looked at me.

"And there is this," I said, and handed him Howard Selby's receipt.

This he studied, then placed it on top of the statement.

"Smells very strongly of blackmail," he said. "Could get you fifteen years."

"That's a fact. Could get her twenty years in a smelly Italian jail, could get Pofferi the same, could get you five years for harbouring dangerous criminals."

He reached in a box and took out a Havana cigar. He bit off the end, spat, then lit up carefully.

"What had you in mind, Mr. Anderson?"

"She told you. Let's have some action. Breathing the same air as you, Diaz, is bad for my health."

He blew smoke at me.

"She mentioned a hundred thousand," he said, his eyes glittering. "I told her that was bluff."

"Call it, and see what happens. It's a hundred thousand or I blow the whistle."

"And land in jail."

"It won't come to that. She'll find the money. I have an ace against your king." I leaned forward to stub out my cigarette in his ash tray. "Think about it. How much has she raised already?"

"Enough to pay you off if you play smart."

"How much?"

"Fifty thousand."

I shook my head.

"One hundred is better."

He opened a drawer in his desk and began to put packets of $100 bills in front of me. He made a line of five packets. Then again from the drawer he took out a leather document case.

"Fifty thousand, Mr. Anderson, and I will throw in this very fine case," he said.

I stared at the money and felt my hands turn clammy. I had never seen so much money in one lump, and the sight of all that green really turned me on.

"Seventy-five," I said, my voice a croak.

"Fifty, Mr. Anderson. Act smart. She's scraped the barrel."

He began putting the packets into the document case and I just sat there, hypnotized. I knew I should bargain, but I also knew I hadn't really believed it would be as easy as this: I didn't really believe I would get anything. I had dreamed of laying my hands on big money, but up to this moment, I knew I had been kidding myself. Now, here I was being handed fifty thousand dollars! I could scarcely believe it.

He pushed the loaded case across his desk towards me.

"Don't come back for more, Mr. Anderson," he said, his voice soft, his eyes menacing. "Blackmailers are greedy, but this is the final payment. Okay?"

"Yes," I said, and pushed back my chair.

"I promise you one thing, Mr. Anderson, if you try to put pressure on again, you will have an unpleasant end. I, personally, will take care of you. You will die slowly. Okay?"

I felt a chill run up my spine as our eyes locked. I have a dread of snakes, and right now, Diaz looked like a snake.

"You have yourself a deal," I said. "Keep clear of me and I'll keep clear of you." I got to my feet, picked up the document case, then walked to the door. I paused and looked at him. "Was it you who killed Pete and the boy?"

He gave me a bored stare.

"Why should you care?" he asked, and began putting my statement back in its envelope.

I left him, crossed the bar and out into the hot sunshine. My one thought was to get this money into safe-keeping. I drove fast to my bank, rented an individual safe, took from the document case five one hundred dollar bills and locked the rest away.

It was as I was about to head for home, I remembered Joey. I drove back to the waterfront, parked the car and walked fast to *Lobster Court*. I had to knock several times on Joey's door before he opened up. He was wearing a pair of underpants and he looked sleepy.

"Did I wake you, Joey?" I said, moving into the room.

"It's okay, Mr. Anderson."

"Jimbo still on the job?"

"Yes, Mr. Anderson."

"The job's finished, Joey. Call him off. I don't want them watched any more." I took out my wallet and gave him a $50 bill. "Okay?"

His eyes brightened.

"Gee! Thanks Mr. Anderson! You don't want me to report any more?"

"That's right. Forget it, will you, Joey?"

He gave me an odd, sly smile.

"I don't forget, Mr. Anderson. They killed Tommy."

"Yeah, I know, but forget them. They are dangerous. Keep away from them. Okay?"

He smiled again.

"You look after your business, Mr. Anderson. Me and Jimbo will look after ours."

"Now, wait a minute. Leave them alone! You can't do anything to that bunch. They are in the big league."

He stared at me for a long moment, then nodded.

"Just as you say, Mr. Anderson."

"That's my boy!" I slapped him on his shoulder and went down the rickety stairs three at a time.

As I headed for home, I thought of all that green stuff stashed away in the bank. I could scarcely believe a snake like Diaz would have parted so easily. Well, he had parted, and I was rich!

This called for a celebration. Bertha and I would go out on the town! I looked at the dashboard clock. The time was close to 19.00. She would be back home by now. If she had a date, she would have to break it.

Leaving the Maser outside the highrise, I took the express elevator to my floor, unlocked the front door and hurried in. As I shut the door, the telephone bell began to ring.

Bertha! I grinned to myself. She could smell money two hundred miles away.

I snatched up the receiver.

"Hi, baby!"

A cool, detached voice, snooty and feminine, said, "Is that Mr. Bart Anderson?"

"Sure. Who is it?"

"Hold a moment. Mr. Mel Palmer wants to speak to you."

Before I could think of a reason why I didn't want to speak to him, there was a click, and Palmer came on the line.

"I have been trying to contact you, Mr. Anderson," he said plaintively.

"Right now, Mr. Palmer, I am on vacation," I said briskly. "If it's anything important, will you call the office?"

"Mr. Anderson, I have given Mr. Hamel your report and he is satisfied, but he wants to talk to you personally."

I blinked, then asked, "What about, Mr. Palmer?"

He heaved a sigh that came over the line like a death rattle.

"Mr. Anderson, if I could fathom every whim or

request Mr. Hamel inflicts on me, I would be less neurotic that I am. All I know is he wants to see you at his place at ten o'clock tomorrow morning."

"Tell him I'm on vacation," I said, just to make life harder for him.

"Mr. Anderson! Please be there. Mr. Hamel is expecting you."

"What's in it for me?"

"What was that?"

"I'll be breaking into my vacation so I will be working again. I don't work for nothing."

He gave a soft moan.

"Do I have to do this through Miss Kerry?"

"Send me a personal cheque for a hundred dollars, Mr. Palmer, and there's no problem."

"Very well. Can I tell Mr. Hamel to expect you?"

"You can bet your sweet life you can," I said, and hung up.

Man! I thought, the green is rolling in. I dialled Bertha's number. When she answered, I said, "Hi, gorgeous! Guess who's calling?"

"Oh, you! Where's the money I lent you?"

"Is that all you think about . . . money?"

"Where is it?"

"Honey, relax. We're going to celebrate tonight. Hold onto your bra straps. I'm going to take you to the Spanish Bay grill. How's that?"

"Are you drunk?" Bertha demanded.

"Not yet, but we will be, and another thing, baby, I've been looking at my big double bed. It looks lonely."

She giggled.

"Just tell me, Bart, have you got my money?"

"I've got it, baby. How about filling the second pillow?"

"The Spanish Bay grill?"

"That's it."

"Do you know what they charge for a dinner I'm going to eat?"

"I know."

"This I can't believe. Have you robbed a bank?"

"I'll give you one hour. If you're not here in one hour, I'm calling another dolly bird."

"Those pattering feet you are hearing running down the corridor to your door are mine," and she hung up.

I replaced the receiver and cried Yip-hee!

Man! I said. Isn't money beautiful!

*　　*　　*

After four champagne cocktails, I was reckless enough to confide in Bertha. We were sitting in the super-duper restaurant of the Spanish Bay grill, and we had ordered a meal that made even Bertha's eyes pop.

"How are you going to pay for it, Bart?" she asked. I believed she was anticipating the cops being called after we had eaten.

So I told her. I didn't go into the small print, but I told her part of the story.

"The fact is, baby, Nancy Hamel hasn't been behaving herself. By following her around I have opened a can of worms."

Bertha stared.

"That prissy? What's she been doing?"

"Never mind. I chatted her up. I produced the evidence. She didn't hesitate. She said she would buy the evidence and for me to forget it. What could I do? I obliged the lady."

Bertha patted my hand.

"I always knew that one day, kiddo, you would get smart. How much?"

"Fifty thousand bucks."

The moment I said it, I regretted it, but the last cocktail was enough to push me over the edge of caution.

Bertha released a squeal that made everyone in the grillroom turn and stare.

"For God's sake!" I said feverishly. "Remember where you are."

"Fifty thousand dollars?" she hissed, leaning forward to gape at me.

"Yep!"

The waiter came forward to serve the caviar.

"Fifty thousand dollars!" Bertha repeated as soon as the waiter had gone. "What are you going to do with all that money?"

"You and I are going on vacation, baby. It's time we relaxed. I'm thinking of hiring a yacht and drifting in the sun. Want to come?"

"Try and stop me! Honey, leave this to me. I have gentlemen friends. I know a fink with a gorgeous yacht, and I can talk him into letting us have it for practically nothing. Four crew, a French chef, a butler and the food!" She rolled her eyes. "For how long?"

"Now wait a minute. That sounds expensive."

"How long?"

"Four weeks: no more."

"I know he's chartered that yacht for twenty thousand a week," Bertha said. "I'll bet my panties I can get it for twenty thousand for four weeks. Imagine!"

I stared suspiciously at her.

"How do you do that?"

"He's a kink. All I have to do is toss off my clothes and dance around his apartment while he sits and drools."

"For that he'll let us have his yacht for four weeks for twenty thousand?"

"Well, he'll expect a few extras, but it's all sex by remote control. Nothing for you to worry about."

"Okay. It's a deal. When do we take off?"

The salmon in aspic arrived.

"I'll see him tomorrow and fix it."

"Are you sure you can?"

She winked at me.

"Want to bet?"

"I may be rich, but I'm not stupid," I said.

*   *   *

At 09.45 the following morning, feeling jaded, I pulled up before the pole barrier that guarded the Paradise Largo estates. The guard came out of his thatched roof cabin and walked majestically towards me.

I regarded him as he came: a big, red faced Mick, around fifty, with weight lifting shoulders and a belly on him that a Japanese wrestler might envy. There was something familiar about him, then I recognized him: Mike O'Flagherty, who once worked as one of Parnell's operators. He had retired a month after I had joined the outfit.

"For Pete's sake, Mike," I said. "Remember me?"

"Bart Anderson!" He shoved a big hairy hand through the open window and nearly dislocated my fingers. "How's the boy?"

"What the hell are you doing here, dressed up like a Christmas tree?"

He grinned.

"Big deal, Bart. When I quit the Agency, I got myself a real softie. I'm one of the guards here. Nothing to do except make people's lives miserable. I lean with my weight, make with the importance, and get paid for it."

"When my time comes, sounds the job for me. Is there a waiting list?"

He laughed.

"Wouldn't suit you, pal. This is strictly snob-land. What brings you here?"

"Mr. Russ Hamel. I have a date with him at ten."

O'Flagherty's eyes popped.

"Is that right? Mr. Hamel is one of our most important clients. Stick around, Bart. I'll check."

"What's with the checking? Lift the pole and let me in."

He shook his head.

"I'll tell you something. This largo is the safest most secure spot in the whole of Florida. No one — repeat no one — goes past that pole without being checked, and without an appointment. No kidnapping, no break and entry, no nothing for the mugs. I'd lose my job if I didn't check you out even though I know who and what you are."

"Don't tell me you check in and out the residents?"

"That would lose me my job." He spat. "Man! The creeps and the bitches who live here turn my stomach! I know everyone of them, know their car numbers. When I see them, up goes the pole. If I keep them waiting, they yell at me, but strangers . . . no!"

"Nice to be that rich."

He grunted, and went back into the guardhouse. After a few minutes, he lifted the pole.

"Go ahead. First avenue to your left. Third gate to your right. There's a T.V. scanner at the gate. Get out of your car, hold up your driving licence, press the red button and wait. After you've waited until some goddamn butler has buttoned his pants, you'll get in."

"Some security," I said as I set the Maser in motion.

O'Flagherty spat.

"You can say that again."

I followed his directions and pulled up outside fifteen foot high, solid oak, nail encrusted gates. Getting out of the car, I pressed the red button on the gate post, held up my driving licence and waited. After a minute or so, the gates swung open: an impressive piece of security. Anyone planning to burglarize the Hamel residence would end in bitter frustration.

I drove up the sand covered drive, shaded by citrus trees, and to a de-luxe ranch style house where a black man in tropical whites stood before the open front door.

I parked the Maser beside a Ford station wagon, got out and walked up the three steps.

"Morning, Mr. Anderson," the black man said with a stiff little bow. "Mr. Hamel is expecting you. This way if you please."

I followed him into a big lobby decorated in warm brown and orange, along a short corridor, out onto a patio where a big fountain in a bigger marble bowl, tossed water into the hot, humid air. Tropical fish swam lazily, looking well fed and smug. There were lounging chairs, glass top tables for when the sun went down. On we went, back into the house, down a passage to a door. Here the black man paused, rapped, then stood aside, opening the door.

"Mr. Anderson, sir," he said, and motioned me forward.

All very impressive, rich, big wheel stuff. I am easily impressed by the show of money, so I was impressed.

"Come in, Mr. Anderson," a voice called: a hearty, baritone of a voice of a man who is very sure of himself.

I entered the big air-conditioned room. It was a room I immediately envied: comfortable, intimate with lounging chairs, big settees, occasional tables, a big desk, teak polished floor with rich looking rugs, well stocked cocktail cabinet, tape recorders and an I.B.M. C82 typewriter on a typing table. A big picture window gave onto a lush lawn that sloped down to the canal.

Behind the desk sat Russ Hamel. He was just like his photograph: square faced, heavily built, tanned and handsome. He got to his feet and extended his hand.

"Good of you to come, Mr. Anderson. I hear you are on vacation."

I made noises as we shook hands. He waved me to a chair.

"Coffee? A drink? A cigar?"

"Nothing right now, thank you sir." I sat down.

"I've read your report." He tapped the report lying on his desk. "I bet you have no idea why I hired you to watch my wife."

I looked straight at him, giving him my modified cop stare.

"That's an easy one, Mr. Hamel. You wanted authentic material for the book you're writing so you wrote yourself some poison-pen letters, instructed your agent to hire us, picked on Mrs. Hamel as a stooge and asked me to come along so you could see what a shamus looks and acts like."

He gaped at me, then threw back his head and burst out

laughing. Right then I liked the guy: I really liked him.

"Well, for God's sake! And I thought I was being smart. How did you find out?"

"I'm a private detective, Mr. Hamel. It's my job to find out things like that as it's your job to write very successful books."

"You're spot on, Mr. Anderson. I got stuck wondering how an Agency works." He grinned. "Your report has been most valuable. Now would you mind telling me about yourself? I'd like to put you in my book."

"I don't mind, sir."

"I won't be wasting your time, Mr. Anderson. I pay for any material I collect."

Man! I thought. Is this my golden age!

"That's fine with me, sir. What do you want to know?"

We spent the next half hour, talking, or rather I did most of the talking, while he shot questions at me. He wanted to know about the organization of the Agency, the training of operators, my own background: all intelligent questions.

Finally, he nodded.

"Well, thanks, Mr. Anderson. You've given me just what I want." He reached for my lengthy report. "But this is what I really wanted." He regarded me with a smile. "This report of yours is not only of value for the book I'm writing, but it is more than valuable to me in my personal life."

"Is that right?" I said blankly.

"My plot revolves around a woman married to a busy surgeon. She is considerably younger than he is," Hamel said. "He gets poison-pen letters about his wife so he has her watched. This is a tale of jealousy. The detective turns in a report that matches yours. The surgeon's wife leads a blameless, lonely life. The reason why I decided to use my wife as a guinea-pig is because I know for certain she also leads a blameless, lonely life." He smiled. "I wasn't taking any risks. I was sure, as I am sitting here, you would turn in a report like this one."

I looked away.

Man! I thought, if you only knew what a can of worms you have opened, you wouldn't be sitting there with that wide, confident smile on your face!

"I'm grateful to you, Mr. Anderson," he went on, "for such a detailed report. I didn't realize how dull and lonely my wife's life has been while I have been locked away writing this book. That is going to be altered."

I didn't say anything. What was there to say?

"Thanks for your time, Mr. Anderson." He produced a sealed envelope which he handed to me, then stood up. "Accept this as a fee."

"Thank you, Mr. Hamel," I said, and he conducted me to the door.

His black servant was waiting.

"So long," Hamel said, shook hands and retired back to his room.

In the Maser, I lit a cigarette and wondered how long it would be before Hamel discovered he had married a murderess. With any luck, he might never know. I hoped he wouldn't. I liked the guy. I liked him still more, when opening the envelope he had given me, I found I was $500 the richer.

CHAPTER SIX

Nothing lasts for ever, but while it lasted, it had been a technicolour dream. As I lay on the sun deck with Bertha by my side, I looked back on those four gorgeous, lush-plush weeks we had spent on this super-duper yacht.

Bertha had fixed it to charter the yacht for $20,000, the round trip, but there had been a catch in it. Whether she didn't give out enough or the Fink's demands made her draw a line, he agreed she could have the yacht, but she would have to foot the check for the crew, the food and the drink. As she was spending my money, she agreed. When she broke the news, I thought of all that green stuff I now owned and remembered what my father once had said: *Never act like a piker, even if you are one*. So I said okay . . . what's money for?

We had visited Caman Islands, Bermuda, the Bahamas and Martinique. We had swum, eaten the best food money could provide, drank four bottles of champagne every day, plus a continuous supply of rum punches that had made Bertha so sexy I had trouble to supply the demand. We entertained the usual scroungers who always invade luxury yachts when they tie up.

We had a ball, but nothing lasts forever.

We were now heading back to Paradise City and would arrive this evening.

"Are you packed, honey?" I asked, stretching.

"Don't spoil it. I don't want this ever to end."

"Me too, but we'd better pack." I got to my feet. "I'll pack first, you next, huh?"

"Go away!"

I went down to the state cabin and looked around. Man! Was I going to miss all this! Reluctantly, I took a suitcase from the closet and tossed it on the bed.

There came a knock on the door, and the Chief steward-cum-butler-cum-valet entered.

He was tall, lean with a hatchet shaped face and beady eyes as animated as sea washed pebbles. His service to us had been immaculate, but all the time he was with us, he looked as if there was a faint, unpleasant smell under his thin nostrils.

"I will be happy to do that for you, sir. You will be leaving us I believe this evening?"

"Yeah. That's a good idea. Pack for me, and pack for Mrs. Anderson."

For the sake of decency, we had come aboard as husband and wife, but I had the idea that we weren't conning this guy, nor the Captain, nor the rest of the crew.

"Yes, sir." He paused, then produced a fat envelope. "Here is the accounting, sir. It is usual to settle before we land."

"Sure," I said. "I'll fix that."

"It is also usual to distribute twenty-five per cent of the total amongst the crew, sir. I will be happy to do this for you."

I looked at him and he looked at me.

"Twenty-five per cent?"

He allowed his thin lips to part in a smile.

"Well, of course, sir, if you wish to increase the amount . . ."

"Sure . . . sure," and I left him and went into the saloon. Sitting down at the desk, I opened the envelope and regarded the account. The total came to $36,000. The Chief Steward had added in pencil $9,000 for tooking: final total $45,000. I sucked in a long, slow breath. Then I went through the items. Then I sat back. After more staring at the account, I took out my pencil and did a little figuring. I came to the conclusion that I was now worth two thousand, three hundred dollars, after having had over fifty thousand dollars four weeks ago.

I walked to the sun deck where Bertha was pouring

yet another glass of champagne.

"That was quick," she said. "Don't tell me you've packed already."

"Prune-face is doing it. He's doing yours too."

She stretched, smiling.

"This is the life, Bart, Hmmm, lovely."

"Yeah. Take a close look."

I handed her the misery. She spent a few minutes going through the items, then shrugged and handed the accounts back to me.

"It was worth it. I don't regret a dime."

My money, of course, not hers.

"This practically puts me back in hock again, baby."

"Well, you still have your job."

"Yeah. I still have my job."

She poured me champagne and patted the mattress.

"Don't look so down in the mouth, pet. Money is for spending."

I sat beside her. I was now thinking what a bird brain I had been to have accepted fifty thousand dollars from Snake Diaz. I hadn't even pressed him. I had asked for one hundred thousand, and had let him fob me off with half! Man! How stupid can you be? I thought. I had had that snake over a barrel, and I had let him get away with it. Then I remembered what he had said: *Don't come back for more. Blackmailers are greedy. This is the final payment. Okay?* Then he had said: *I promise you one thing, if you try to put the pressure on again, you will have an unpleasant end. I, personally, will take care of you. You will die slowly.*

What a mug! I thought. Well, that's it. I'm not taking any more chances with that snake. He means just what he said.

"Bart!" Bertha said sharply. "Tell me something: how bad is this can of worms you've opened?"

"Couldn't be worse."

"She paid fifty thousand to keep it quiet without a struggle?"

"Well, not quite, but she paid."

"You went to the wrong customer, Bart. You shouldn't have gone to her."

I stared at her.

"You don't know what you're saying."

"Did you or did you not get the money from Nancy Hamel?"

"I worked through her agent, but she found the money."

"If the can is as bad as you say it is, you could have asked much more, couldn't you?"

"She hadn't any more."

Bertha nodded.

"That's where you made your big mistake. You should have gone to Russ Hamel who is worth millions."

"You don't know the set-up, honey."

She lit a cigarette.

"Then tell me."

"Bertha, you don't want to get involved in this."

She looked hard at me.

"Tell me!"

"It's safer for you to keep out of it!"

"Stop acting like a virgin who sees it for the first time! Tell me!"

So I told her. As I talked, I felt a sense of relaxation. I needed to confide in someone. It wasn't until I started from the beginning: watching Nancy, Josh Jones, running into Pofferi, Pete and Tommy, then Coldwell with his mug shots, and finally Diaz with his threat, that I realized just how much I needed to confide.

Bertha listened. When I got up to the part about Nancy being Lucia Pofferi, she sat up, staring at me, but she said nothing until I had finished.

"You really mean Nancy Hamel is Lucia whatever her name is: a murderess?" Bertha asked, her voice low.

"No doubt about it."

She ran her fingers through her hair, closed and opened her eyes.

106

"Man!" she whispered.

"Yeah. I told you. So okay, now you know. The weak hinge is that if it ever surfaces, I'll spend years in jail."

"And you sold this package to Diaz for fifty thousand?"

"I've told you!" I snapped. "Okay, I wanted a hundred, but when he put all that green on his desk, I fell for it."

"Man!" She cupped her breasts and moaned softly.

"Okay. Okay, don't tell me. I should have twisted his goddamn arm, but he's dangerous. He said she had scraped the barrel."

"But there was nothing he could have done to you!" Bertha hissed. "You had him! He couldn't touch you with that report with Selby! Bart! You had him, and you let him jump off the hook!"

I wiped the sweat off my face.

"I've been telling myself that again and again, but I did it!"

Lowering her voice and putting her hand on my arm, she said, "You still have another hook and a much bigger fish."

I stared at her.

"Now, look, honey, I'm all through. I got fifty grand. We've enjoyed it, and we've spent it. That's it. I'm back in hock again, and I start work on Monday." I paused and gave her a double take. "What hook? What fish?"

She gave an exasperated sigh.

"There are times, Bart, when I really and truly think you need your head examined. You should never have gone to Nancy. You should have known she would have rushed to Pofferi. By trying to put the pressure on her, you come against Diaz."

"I know that now," I said angrily. "I thought I had a soft touch. Well, it paid off, didn't it?"

"Did it? What have you left?"

"What hook? What fish? Spell it out!"

"Russ Hamel! You should have gone to him in the first place. Can't you see that? Take a look at Hamel, Bart. Take a close look. Here is a big selling writer, getting long in the tooth, and rolling in money. He meets up with Nancy and falls for her. He sees in her his second chance. Bear that in mind, Bart. *His second chance*. He found out his first wife was a tramp. That must have dented his ego. He got rid of her. Now he marries a young woman he thinks blameless. Think how he would react if someone tells him she is one of the most wanted Italian terrorists with two murders behind her. How do you imagine he would react?"

"You're doing the talking," I said, leaning forward. "You tell me."

"This man is world famous. The scandal and the uproar if the press got hold of this would be like an atomic bomb going off. A man with his imagination would flip his lid, but, apart from doing everything to keep this quiet, he would want to protect his wife. He would think her past was behind her. He would believe she loved him as he loves her. He would do anything — repeat — anything to keep her out of an Italian jail."

"Would he if he finds out she is married to Pofferi? That could sour it."

"How do you know she's married to Pofferi? It's only what the Italian police say, isn't it?"

"There's that, but why should they say so if she isn't?"

Bertha made an exasperated gesture.

"You're getting away from the point! The point is you can bet that Hamel will pay to have this swept under the rug whether she's married to Pofferi or not."

I thought about this and began to get a little excited. A man like Hamel just wouldn't want his public to know he had been taken for a sucker. I was willing to bet on that.

"And listen, Bart, don't let this fish jump off the hook. He's good for at least a million."

I gaped at her.

"A million! You're out of your mind!"

"He's rolling in money. What's a million to a man like him . . . chick feed."

"Wait a minute. He might turn ugly, babe. He might

call the cops, and then where would I be?"

"Then where would he be? Where would Nancy be?" Bertha said. "You have him, Bart. It's a cinch."

And listening to her, suddenly thinking of what it would mean to own a million dollars, I kidded myself it *was* a cinch.

The first thing I did when I returned to my apartment was to call Howard Selby. I told him I was back from vacation.

"Keep that envelope, Howard," I said. "I'm back on the job again. I'll call you every week to tell you I'm still alive. Okay?"

"Sounds as if you're up against a tough bunch," Selby said. "Do you think they mean business?"

"No, but I'm taking no chances. Thanks, pal," and I hung up.

I poured myself a Scotch and sat down. Bart, baby, I said to myself, here's where you exercise your smart brain. I had been away from Paradise City for four weeks. I had been out of touch with any developments. Suppose Pofferi had been caught? Suppose Coldwell had found out who Nancy was? Man! Would I look a stupe trying to bite Hamel's ear if that had happened! I sweated a little just to think of it. I could almost hear the clang of the cell door.

The quickest and easiest way to check would be to go once again to the *Paradise City Herald*'s morgue. I looked at my watch. The time was 19.40. Fanny Battley would be on duty. Finishing my drink, I went down to the Maser.

"My! What a tan!" Fanny exclaimed as I walked into the morgue. "Did you have a good time?"

"You can say that again." I rested my hands on her desk and leaning forward, gave her my sexy smile. "It all went too fast. When are you going, Fan?"

"Next month. I'm going to my folks in Georgia." She sighed. "A duty visit."

"Yeah, I know. Well, what's new? Any excitements?"

"Nothing much. A few Big Wheels down here on

vacation and throwing their weight around. No, can't say any excitements."

"Nor crimes?"

"A couple of break-ins, but they were caught: hippies. A jerk tried to hold up the Casino. He lasted two minutes. I think that's about all."

I relaxed. If Pofferi had been caught, Fanny would certainly know about it.

"The same old City, huh?"

"I guess. There was a horrid hit-and-run case the night before last. Penny Highbee."

I stiffened.

"The attorney's wife?"

"Yes. A drunk driver. She was getting into her car, and this car came from nowhere and slammed into her. Two witnesses saw it. They said the car was swerving like crazy."

I felt a prickle run up my spine.

"Hurt bad?"

"She died on the way to hospital."

"Jesus!" I found my mouth dry. "Have they caught the driver?"

"Have they?" Fanny snorted. "Neither of the witnesses got the number, and one swears it was a blue car, the other a green."

Nancy Hamel's best and closest friend! I thought. Did it mean anything?

"We've given her a big write-up," Fanny went on. "Do you want to see it?"

"No, I guess not." I looked at my watch. "I guess I'll get moving. I start work on Monday."

"We all have to do it." As I began to move, she went on, "There was that little Indian boy they fished out of the harbour, but he wouldn't interest you, would he?"

I felt my heart give a lurch.

"What little Indian boy?"

"Just one of the kids on the waterfront. The cops reckoned he slipped and hit his head and fell in."

110

"What's his name, Fan?"

She gave a quick glance, but true to her reputation, she didn't begin to ask questions. She got up and went to the card index, searched, then said, "Jimbo Osceola. He lived at Lobster Court."

"When was this?"

"Last night."

"Thanks, Fan," and leaving her looking puzzled, I returned to the Maser.

I had an instinctive feeling that the deaths of Penny Highbee and Jimbo were connected with Nancy and Pofferi. I sat in the car and brooded. Could be, I told myself, that Penny Highbee had begun to suspect that Nancy wasn't all she appeared to be. The two women were close friends. Maybe, Nancy had let the mask slip. Pofferi wouldn't hesitate to put an end to Penny if there was the slightest suspicion she might blow Nancy's cover.

I had warned Joey to keep clear of Diaz. Remembering his sly smile when he said he would, I now felt sure he hadn't heeded my warning. Jimbo had got too close, and they had spotted him as they had spotted Tommy.

Where was Joey?

I felt an urgent need to talk to him. I drove down to the waterfront, parked the Maser and walked fast to *Lobster Court*. The usual bunch of kids, kicking a football around, paused in their game to stare at me.

As I headed for Joey's building, one of them called, "Hi, mister."

I paused. A dirty Indian kid of around nine years of age, ran up to me.

"No use looking for Joey, mister."

I took out my handkerchief and wiped my sweating face.

"What do you mean?"

"He doesn't live there no more. He quit last night."

"Where's he gone?"

The kid looked dumb.

"I don't know, mister."

I produced a dollar bill.

"Where's he gone. . ." I repeated.

He stared at the bill with greedy eyes.

"You Mister Anderson, mister?"

"Yeah."

"He didn't tell me where he was going, mister, but he said to tell you the guy was still there."

"You're sure you don't know where he is? I'm a buddy of his. I want to see him."

I produced another dollar bill.

"I don't know. He took the bus. He had a suitcase with him."

"What bus?"

"The Key West bus."

"Okay." I gave him the two dollars. "Listen, if you see him, tell him to telephone me."

The kid grabbed the money and grinned.

"Betcha, mister."

As I headed back to my apartment, I felt worried and lonely. I decided I didn't want to spend the night alone. I changed direction and drove to Bertha's highrise.

I found her still unpacking.

"Why, honey," she exclaimed as she opened the front door. "What's with it? I'm in a hell of a mess."

Although Bertha always looked immaculate, her apartment was always in a perpetual mess, and now, plus half opened suitcases, clothes all over it was in even a worse mess.

"Throw something on, baby," I said. "We'll eat out. I've things to talk about."

She gave me a quick probing stare, then went into her bedroom. She returned, dressed and immaculate in under ten minutes which was a record for her.

"Something happened?"

"Yeah, but it'll keep. We'll go to Chez Louis. We can talk there, and baby, I need a sleeping companion."

"No problem." She hooked her arm in mine. It wasn't until we had reached the Maser that I understood her docile performance. Usually, we would always have an argument about where we were to eat. I gave a wry grin as I helped her into the car. She was already imagining I was worth a million dollars.

It wasn't until we had settled in the small restaurant which was half empty and had ordered blue crab and steaks stuffed with oysters that I told her the news.

Fortified with a champagne cocktail, she listened without popping with her eyes.

"Could be a coincidence," she said when I was through.

"Could be hell! Highbee the night before last. Jimbo last night," I said. "I told you, babe, these guys are lethal."

"They can't do anything to you."

"I hope not."

"Then the sooner you talk to Hamel, the safer it'll be for us to pack and blow."

"I can't talk to him yet."

"Why not?"

"The wife of his attorney and his wife's best friend has died," I explained patiently. "This isn't the moment to get to see him. It's going to be a real job anyway to see him without this complication."

She attacked her crab.

"What's the complication about seeing him?" she asked finally.

"I can't just drop in." I explained to her about the security of Paradise Largo.

"Man! What it is to be rich!" Bertha sighed.

"Sure is. So I'll have to wait for the dust to settle, then I'll try getting him on the 'phone. I'm not going to write . . . that's evidence if it turns sour."

She continued to eat, but I could see by her frown she was thinking. When she laid down her fork, after making sure there wasn't a morsel left, she said, "Attend the funeral."

"What the hell should I be doing attending Penny Highbee's funeral?"

"Didn't your Agency ever do work for Highbee?"

"Come to think of it, a good dozen jobs."

"So . . . showing the Agency's respects."

"What makes you think Hamel will be there?"

"Bart! If he isn't, it doesn't matter. If he is, you tell him you need to see him urgently. He'll fix a date. Anyway, it's worth a try, isn't it?"

I didn't dig the idea, but decided it would be better than trying to get through on the telephone.

"I don't know where the funeral is to be or where."

"God give me strength!" Bertha moaned. "You're a goddamn detective, aren't you? Find out!"

* * *

Glenda Kerry looked up from the mail spread out on her desk and gave me her cool, impersonal stare.

"Hi, delicious," I said. "Here I am: all ready for work. What's cooking?"

"You have the Solly Herschenheimer stint, starting at midday today."

I stared at her.

"You wouldn't be kidding?"

"They asked for you. Why, I can't imagine. I was going to give it to Chick, but they wanted you."

"Is this good news! Naturally, they wanted me: I'm educated and handsome. Okay, I'll be there dead on the nail."

The Solly Herschenheimer stint, as it was known in the Agency, came around every year. It was the softest job the Agency had ever landed. I never found out what Herschenheimer had to pay, but I was sure it was plenty. That didn't worry me: the job was a push-over and the food out of this world.

Solly Herschenheimer was an enormously wealthy eccentric with a rooted idea that he was in constant danger of being assassinated. No one, including Chief of Police Terrell, was able to convince him otherwise. He refused to name his enemies, and the general opinion was that he was a harmless nut case. He lived like a recluse and employed two bodyguards who were supposed to be on constant watch against an attack. When the time came for one of the bodyguards to take his vacation, the Parnell Agency was called in to supply a substitute. I had been lucky the previous year to get the job, and now, I was getting it again.

The job was a vacation in itself. There was nothing to do except wander around the grounds of the big house, watch T.V. in the evenings and eat enormous luxury meals Herschenheimer's butler, Jarvis, provided. The only drawback to the job was the old nut frowned on liquor, but the guards supplied their own, and no bones were broken.

At the end of two weeks, when the guard returned, the substitute received a $200 took which alone made the job the ambition of all operators working for the Agency. To land this plum twice running was indeed a gift from the gods.

"You know Mr. Herschenheimer has moved residence?" Glenda asked.

"I didn't. Where's he now?"

"Paradise Largo. He's been there for the past three months. That's where you are to report."

I wondered immediately if his new place was near Hamel's residence. With a feeling of excitement, I realized, working on the Largo, could give me the chance of calling on Hamel without attracting attention.

The cards seemed to be falling my way.

"Okay, lovely," I said. "I'll get moving."

I had learned from Fanny Battley that the Highbee funeral was taking place at 10.30. I would have time to attend, and still get to my new job by midday.

As soon as I arrived at the cemetery, I saw that Bertha's idea of contacting Hamel was a non-starter. At a rough guess, there were some three hundred mourners milling around. I waited, trying to look sorrowful, my eyes searching for Hamel. It was only after the burial that I did see him. He was with Nancy who was in total black. He had his arm around her as if supporting her.

I edged my way through the crowd until I was close enough to get a good look at her. What I saw shocked me. She looked like a ghost: white, her eyes sunken, her lips trembling, and tears made her face glisten.

I saw this was no time to ask Hamel for a date. As I began to move away, Nancy suddenly collapsed. Hamel caught her up in his arms and carried her down the pathway between the graves and to a waiting car.

There was a movement in the crowd and a few hushed voices. I watched the car drive away.

"Mr. Anderson . . ."

I turned to find Mel Palmer regarding me.

"A sad occasion, Mr. Anderson." He looked as sad as a man who has picked up a $100 bill. "We all have but a short time to live . . . sad."

"That's right."

"I'm afraid it has upset Mr. Hamel, but fortunately, his book is now finished." Palmer positively beamed. "The book is a major triumph! The best he has ever written!"

"Right now, he seems to have a problem with Mrs. Hamel. She seemed also upset."

"Yes . . . yes." He was obviously not interested in Nancy. "But time is a great healer. She will make new friends."

Spotting someone he knew, he nodded to me and hurried away.

I walked thoughtfully back to where I had parked the Maser. I was puzzled. I was certain Nancy was Lucia Pofferi: a vicious, two-time murderess, and yet I was sure her show of grief wasn't faked. The answer to this oddity could be that Pofferi had given her no inkling he was going to kill the woman who had befriended her, but when the faked accident had happened, Nancy had guessed the truth. This could prove interesting. Would this ruthless act of murder turn her against Pofferi?

I paused as I approached the Maser. I had reason to:

Detective Tom Lepski was sitting in the passenger's seat, his hat tipped over his eyes, a cigarette smouldering in his thin lips.

Trouble? I wondered, and braced myself. I put on my well-what-do-you-know expression and reached the car.

"Hi, Tom."

He pushed his hat to the back of his head and nodded.

"You should always lock your car," he said. "What's the idea attending funerals?"

To give myself time, I walked around the car and slid into the driving seat.

"Highbee's one of our clients," I said as I settled. "The Colonel wanted to show respect. I bought it. What are you doing here?"

"Looking." Lepski scowled. "Between you and me, we don't like this set up. We don't think this guy was so drunk. There is a smell."

"Of what?"

"We are not sure, but it could have been murder. We have a new witness: Ernie Thresher. He lives in an apartment in the highrise Mrs. Highbee was visiting." He paused and looked sharply at me. "This is strictly off the record, Bart. We're keeping Thresher under the wraps until we dig more. He swears this wasn't a drunken accident. He was looking out of his window and saw the killer's car parked at the end of the street. He wondered what the car was doing there. As soon as Mrs. Highbee came out, this car started up and drove like crazy, straight at her. She didn't stand a chance."

I tried to look calmer than I felt.

"Who would want to kill her?" I said.

"That's the problem. All the same, we like Thresher's evidence. The other two witnesses contradict each other. Thresher has given us a description of the car and the number. We've checked. The car was stolen from Harry Dellish, the court reporter, from his garage on the night of this so-called accident. We've found the car, and it has

117

a dented fender. Another interesting thing Thresher claims: the driver was coloured."

Josh Jones! I thought, but kept my face dead-pan.

"So?"

"So nothing so far." Lepski looked disgusted. "It's just a smell, but we're working on it. Maybe, we'll turn up something if we knew why anyone wanted to knock off a nice girl like Penny Highbee."

I felt a cold qualm. I could have told him. I could have told him who had done the job, but I knew, once I started giving information, I would be in trouble.

"Maybe someone getting even with Highbee. As an attorney, he must have enemies."

"We thought of that, but Highbee is sure no coloured man had it in for him." Lepski shrugged. "Well, we're working on it." He flicked his cigarette away, then asked, "And you, Bart? Did you have a good vacation?"

"I'll say. My girl friend has a rich fink who lent her his yacht. Can you imagine: all for free."

He grinned sourly.

"You have a way with women." He brooded, then went on, "Did you hear about this second Indian boy who's been knocked off?"

I put on my for-God's-sake expression.

"I've been out of touch. A second Indian boy?"

"Yeah. Tommy Osceola's brother, Jimbo. Remember? Tommy was shot along with Pete."

"What happened?"

"He was bashed over the head and tossed into the harbour. No one saw a thing." He stared thoughtfully at me. "Something's going on around here, Bart. Ever since Coldwell started this scare about Pofferi, we have had three murders and a suspect murder. I keep wondering if Pofferi is behind it all, but then I ask myself why a goddamn Italian terrorist should want to knock off an old drunk, two Indian kids, and Penny Highbee."

"You have a problem." I looked at my watch. "I've got to go, Tom. Guess what? I've landed the Herschenheimer job again. Can I drive you any place?"

"I've got my car." Lepski slid out of the Maser. "The Herschenheimer job? Is that old nut still needing guards?"

"He sure is: a sweet softie."

"See you, and Bart, if you get any ideas about this set-up, pass them on. We need help."

He left me and walked to where he had parked his car.

I wiped my face with my handerchief. I didn't have to spell it out to myself. If I had alerted Coldwell where Pofferi had been hiding, four people would still be alive, but by keeping my mouth shut, I had picked up $50,000. The thought gave me a qualm, then I thought that by still keeping my mouth shut, I stood a sweet chance of picking up a million dollars.

Bart, baby, I said to myself, this isn't the time to develop a conscience. You don't pick up a million if you start considering other people. Remember what your old man used to say: *A shut mouth is a wise mouth*.

So be wise, Bart, baby, be wise.

I started the engine and drove away from the smell of funeral flowers and headed for Paradise Largo.

Mike O'Flagherty welcomed me at the guardhouse.

"You got the job?" he said, grinning. "I was told an operator from Parnell's was coming. Brother! Have you picked a sweet one!"

"Do I know it! Where do I find the old nut's place?"

"Right opposite Mr. Hamel's residence." Mike leaned against the Maser. "I'm real sorry for Mrs. Hamel. She lost her best friend in a car smash. She's just back from the funeral: in a bad way. Dr. Hirsch was called. He arrived just five minutes ago. I like that lady. She's real nice."

"Yeah," I said, and wondered how he would react if I told him who Nancy really was. "I've got to get on, Mike. I don't want to be late."

"Sure." He raised the pole and I drove under it and to Hamel's place. Right opposite was another set of high gates. I rang the bell and the gates swung back.

Carl Smith, one of the guards who I had met the last time I had been on the job, shook hands.

"Glad to see you, Bart," he said. He was a big, fair, youngish man with freckles and a wide smile. "I was hoping they would send you."

"How's the old nut?"

"Just the same. Not causing any trouble. You eaten yet?"

"I was betting on lunch here."

"You've won. Lunch will be in ten minutes."

"Jarvis still with you?"

"You bet, and the chef's as good as ever."

Leaving the car under the shade of the trees, we walked together to a cottage type of building. Beyond it, I could see the main residence. It was big: at least a sixteen bedroom house.

"We work here," Carl said, indicating the cottage. "No problem. We just sit and enjoy ourselves. No one can get on the Largo without authorization. The old nut doesn't realize that otherwise we'd lose our jobs. No one is going to tell him." He laughed. "Your hours, Bart, are from midday to midnight, then midnight to midday on alternate days. Okay?"

"Suits me."

We went into the cottage. It consisted of one big room. Upstairs were two bedrooms and a bathroom. The sitting-room was equipped with lounging chairs, a desk, and a T.V. set.

"The one thing missing is the bar," I said, looking around.

Carl winked. He went to the desk and produced a bottle of Scotch. Going to a cupboard, he disclosed a small refrigerator.

"We have to look after ourselves, Bart," he said. "Have a drink?"

While he was fixing the drinks, I went over to the window and looked across at the shut gates. I could just make out the top of Hamel's roof. There was a big tree with spreading branches near the entrance to the Herschenheimer residence. I reckoned if I got up in those branches I would be able to look directly into Hamel's garden and house.

Turning, I took the glass Carl offered me.

Yes, I told myself, the cards are certainly falling my way.

CHAPTER SEVEN

As soon as we had eaten an excellent lunch, Carl took himself off. I sat under the trees where I could see the house and the entrance gates, and made myself comfortable. I had Hamel on my mind. I now knew he had finished his book, and I remembered Palmer saying Hamel would pick up over eleven million dollars when the book was finished. So Hamel couldn't plead poverty when I put on the bite. My thought now was when to bite him. Nancy had collapsed. Maybe this wasn't the right time to approach Hamel. Maybe I had better wait. At the back of my mind, I knew I was kidding myself. It wasn't because Hamel was having trouble with his wife that I was going to wait, it was because I was uneasy about putting pressure on him. He was nobody's push-over. He was a toughie. He could tell me to go to hell, or even worse, call the cops, or do something desperate. I had an uneasy feeling he wouldn't dig blackmail.

My mind shifted to Bertha, and I grimaced. I now regretted I had confided in her. She was now smelling a million dollars, and she wouldn't stop nagging me until I did put on the bite.

I then went into my usual technicolour dream of owning a million dollars. This time, I swore to myself, when I got the money, I wouldn't spend like crazy. I would buy stock for my old age, and live on the income, but even as I swore, I knew the million would vanish as quickly as Diaz's fifty thousand had vanished. Money just wouldn't stay with me.

Getting bored with my thoughts, I took a walk around the big garden. The flowers, the lawns, the shrubs were immaculate. A Chinese gardener, who looked like Judge

122

Dee, was wagging his long beard over a bed of begonias. He gave me a squinting look of disinterest and returned to his beard wagging.

The big swimming pool looked inviting, but lonely. I wondered if Herschenheimer ever used it. I doubted it. He would probably think someone might jump out of the bushes and drown him.

I saw Jarvis, Herschenheimer's butler, coming down the path towards me. Jarvis could have stepped out of the pages of *Gone with the Wind*. He was the most dignified old negro I have ever seen: tall, very thin, with crinkly white hair, large black eyes and heavy white eyebrows. He would have gladdened the heart of Scarlett O'Hara and the rest of her ilk. I had come to know him well when I last did this job, and I had found that he had an insatiable thirst for crime stories. He would sit for hours, listening to my lies, believing every yarn I dreamed up, with me the central, daring hero, to be true. In return, he provided me with splendid food, and often a box of cigars he had filched from his master.

His old face lit up with a wide smile when he saw me.

"What a pleasure, Mr. Anderson," he said, shaking hands. "I asked for you, but Miss Kerry wasn't sure you would be back from your vacation. I'm so glad. Did you have an enjoyable time?"

As we walked back to the cottage, I told him about the yacht, and about Bertha. He had heard from me about Bertha on my previous stint. I told him Bertha worked for the CIA, so anything I even hinted at about her, he absorbed with wide eyed interest.

When I ran out of telling him lies about my own adventures, I switched to Bertha who, according to me, made Mata Hari look like a convent novice.

We settled in the shade outside the cottage, and he began questioning me about what I had been doing. Having just read a Hadley Chase thriller, I outlined the plot to him, with me as a central character. When I had concluded, an hour later, he got reluctantly to his feet.

"You live a most remarkable life, Mr. Anderson," he said. "I must now attend to Mr. Herschenheimer's tea. I have invited Mr. Washington Smith to have dinner with me at seven. Perhaps you would join us? Mr. Smith is Mr. Hamel's butler. He comes over here during his hours off. He is a pleasant, weil-spoken man."

"Sure," I said. "Glad to."

"I'll arrange to have the meal served in the cottage. It will be more convenient for you to keep an eye on possible intruders," and he gave me a bass laugh to show he was joking.

When he returned to the house, I walked down to the big tree by the entrance gates. It was screened from the house by other trees. I had no trouble swinging myself up to the lower branches, and from there, climbed up and up, until I was overlooking the high hedge that surrounded the Hamel residence.

Sitting astride a branch with my back to the tree trunk, I looked down into the Hamel garden and the ranch style house.

The Ferrari and the Ford wagon stood on the tarmac before the house. There was no sign of life. I sat there for the next two hours, but no one appeared. The house might have been empty.

At 19.00, Jarvis arrived at the cottage with Hamel's butler.

"Mr. Washington Smith meet Mr. Bart Anderson who is looking after the security of the estate while Mr. Jordan is on vacation," Jarvis said.

Mr. Smith smiled as we shook hands.

"We have met before, Mr. Anderson."

"That's right. Glad to see you again."

A young negro in white wheeled in a trolley, and quickly laid the table while Jarvis poured martini cocktails.

"Hey! I thought the boss didn't dig liquor," I said.

Jarvis smiled.

"There's an old saying, Mr. Anderson, about what the eye doesn't see."

124

"The heart doesn't grieve about," Smith concluded as he reached for a glass.

It was during a good meal of pork chops in chilli sauce that I began to pump Smith.

I said it was sad about Mrs. Highbee. I had been at the funeral, and had seen Mrs. Hamel collapse. How was she?

Smith munched for a few moments, then shook his head.

"She is recovering. Mrs. Highbee was her closest friend. It was a great shock, but she is recovering."

"And Mr. Hamel?" I said, my voice casual. "I found him an impressive personality. He said he was going to use me in his book."

Smith sighed.

"I'm worried about Mr. Hamel. He has never been happy since he took up marriage. I have been with him for the past fifteen years. He made a mistake marrying Mrs. Gloria . . . she was no lady. The divorce distressed him. I thought all would be well when he married Mrs. Nancy." He looked at me. "I don't know a nicer lady. I had every hope that the marriage would be a success, but Mr. Hamel is not happy. I don't understand it."

I could have told him. I remember what Gloria Cort had said: *You'd think a guy who could write that stuff would be good in bed. Was I conned? He's as useless to a woman as boiled spaghetti.*

"Well, he certainly makes money with his books. I guess one can't have everything," I said.

"Yes, indeed. Tomorrow, he goes to Hollywood to discuss the film treatment," Smith said. "The film will bring him a lot of money. Mr. Hamel is most generous. He always gives me and my wife, who does the cooking, a present when he sells a film."

"How about the other staff?" I asked, probing. "Do they get something?"

"We have no other staff. In spite of his wealth, Mr. Hamel likes to live simply. He seldom entertains, and when he does, he hires staff and orders food. It is an easy place to run, and my wife and I are not pressed. He always has cold supper. That is why I am able to grace Mr. Jarvis's excellent table."

"I guess Mrs. Hamel will be going with him to Hollywood? Should take her mind off her loss."

He shook his head.

"No, Mrs. Hamel will stay. It will only be for three or four days. I don't think she feels like mixing with the Hollywood people." He frowned. "They are very special."

Jarvis, who had been listening without interest, broke in, "You must tell us about these two Indian boys who died, Mr. Anderson. I am sure you have theories about them."

"Well, no. Even the police don't understand it," I said, thinking how their eyes would bolt out if I told them the facts. "But I can tell you about this odd business the Agency handled last year," and I launched in to yet another of my made-up cases which kept them on the edges of their chairs until Smith said regretfully he had to get back or his wife would be wondering where he was.

Jarvis also remembered he had to see the old nut to bed. I was left on my own and with my thoughts.

I had learned a lot from Smith. He had confirmed what Gloria Cort had told me: Hamel was impotent. He had told me Hamel would be away for three or four days, leaving Nancy on her own. Hamel being away, gave me time. It would also keep Bertha quiet.

My afternoon hadn't been wasted. I relaxed, and when I relax, my thoughts turn to money. I was still spending a million dollars when Carl arrived to relieve me.

"I bet you were busy," he said, grinning.

"A beautiful dinner," I said. "Man! Is this the job?"

I was getting into bed when the telephone bell rang. For a long moment, I hesitated to answer it, then I lifted the receiver.

"Bart!" Bertha's strident voice hit my eardrum like a sledge hammer.

"Hi, honey," I managed to say.

"What about it?"

"What about what?" Although I knew.

She made a sound a train whistle would envy.

"What's happening? Have you seen him?"

"Relax . . . he's away . . . Hollywood. I have it under control, baby."

"When will he be back?"

"Don't be so goddam anxious. Three or four days. Quiet down, baby. I'm handling this . . . remember?"

"You'd better be. I've sold my apartment, and the furniture. Give with the action, Bart! As soon as he gets back, bite him!"

"You've sold . . .? What the hell are you saying?"

"Who wants to live in this crummy place when we're worth millions?" Bertha demanded. "I had a good offer, so I've sold. Now the action is in your court."

I suppressed a groan.

"Okay, okay. Three or four days. I'll fix it."

"Do that," and she hung up.

*   *   *

Some minutes before midnight, I arrived at the Paradise Largo to begin my night's stint. I stopped to chat up Mike O'Flagherty who was going off duty.

We talked of this and that, then I steered the conversation around to the Hamels.

"Any news of Mrs. Hamel?" I asked as I offered him a cigarette.

"The quack called again today. Mr. Hamel left early this morning. I hear he is going to Hollywood: a film deal."

That was what I wanted to know. Hamel was now on his way to Hollywood.

I found Carl waiting to be relieved. Jarvis had left a stack of sandwiches for me in case I starved during the night.

"There's a bottle of Scotch in my drawer," Carl said. "Help yourself."

When he had gone, I ate the sandwiches, had a couple of drinks, then walked to the tree by the gates. I climbed it, surveyed Hamel's ranch house which was in darkness, and after waiting for more than an hour when nothing happened, I returned to the cottage, lay on the settee and went to sleep. Around five in the morning, I forced myself awake, shaved and showered, and wandered around the garden, trying to look like an energetic guard. At 08.00, Jarvis arrived with coffee, pancakes, maple syrup, grilled sausages and scrambled eggs.

While I ate, he talked. He said that as I would be on duty tomorrow at midday, he would arrange another dinner with Washington Smith. I said that was fine with me.

Carl relieved me at midday. I went swimming, then returned to my apartment and slept until 18.00. I didn't feel like coping with Bertha, so I went to a bar for a drink, then feeling hungry, I headed to where I had parked the Maser. As I was getting into the car, I spotted Gloria Cort coming towards me.

"Hi, there!"

She stopped and regarded me, then she smiled, and came up to the Maser.

"Hi! Where did you spring from?" She leant against the car. Her breasts swung against the flimsy material of her dress.

"I'm about to feed my face," I said. "Any chance of your company? I hate eating alone."

She moved rapidly to the off-side and opened the passenger's door.

"Where?"

"Do you like sea food?"

"I prefer meat. There's a restaurant not far from here: Beef on the Hoof. Know it?"

Just like Bertha. The prices at this restaurant would have startled an oil Sheik.

"Not there," I said firmly. "I know a joint where you can get a steak that sits up on your plate and makes bull noises."

She laughed.

"Well, it was a try." She settled herself beside me and her hand fell into my lap. "Nice car."

I gently removed her hand.

"Not right now, baby . . . later, huh?"

I drove her to the restaurant which was off Paradise Avenue. It had piped music that blew your ears, a lot of action, and the waiters dressed as bull-fighters.

When we had settled and ordered steaks, she leaned back, thrusting her breasts at me.

"Where have you been, handsome?" she asked. "I haven't seen you since you blew into the Alameda."

"I get around. What are you doing, foot loose? Don't you do an act there, or something?"

"Only Saturdays. What do you do?"

"Me? I chase the fast buck, and sometimes catch it. How's Diaz these days?"

She gave me a long, searching look.

"What did you say your name was?"

"Bart Anderson."

She nodded.

"Keep clear of Diaz, Bart."

"I've been told that before."

"Now *I'm* telling you. Keep clear of him."

The steaks arrived and we began to eat.

"If he's that poisonous, what's a nice girl like you doing hooking up with him?"

"Who the hell said I was nice?" She pursed her lips and made a rude noise. "But you're right. Whenever I meet up with a man, sooner or later, I ask myself what I'm doing with him, and I never come up with an answer. The trouble with me is I get infatuated. I got infatuated with that jerk Hamel. Then I got infatuated with this creep Diaz. If I told you how many goddamn finks I've got infatuated with it would take all night."

"Tough," I said. "How's the steak?"

"Marvellous." She started eating again.

So I let her eat. When she finished, she said she would have a sundae with plenty of bananas and cherries. I let her work through that while I drank coffee. When there was nothing more for her to eat, she nodded, pushed back her chair and stood up.

"Let's go," she said. "I'm going to give you a work out. It'll be an experience you'll write up in your diary."

"I don't keep a diary," I said as I paid the check.

"But you will, brother! You certainly will!" Catching hold of my arm, she dragged me out of the restaurant.

*   *   *

The telephone bell brought me awake. I clawed open my eyes and squinted at the bedside clock. It showed 10.05. The sound of the bell pounded my brain. I heard a moan, then a four-letter word, and saw Gloria, half sitting up, naked, beside me.

"Stay still," I croaked. "It's nothing."

I knew it was Bertha, trying to get to me. I had taken a risk, bringing Gloria to my apartment, but she had dangled her sexual equipment so enticingly, I had been swept off my feet.

I have bedded many dolls in my past, but Gloria was something else beside. As a bed partner, she was unique.

I had already told Bertha that I was back to the grindstone, and not to expect to hear from me for a few days, but now Bertha dreamed of sharing my million dollars, she would be hard to shake off.

After a few more rings, the telephone bell sulked into silence.

"Hi," Gloria said, smiling at me. She looked depressingly lively. "That sure was a night, honey."

Feeling boneless, I managed to nod.

"Some coffee. I'll get it." She slid off the bed and ran

naked towards the kitchen. I watched her with carnal appreciation.

After a while, she came back with coffee: strong and reviving. We drank, and I slowly became knitted together. After another cup, this time laced with brandy, my brain began to function. Looking at her, as she sat beside me, I realized she could be useful to me: now was the moment to fish for information.

"Baby," I said. "Tell me about Diaz. Why has he lost his glamour for you?"

"Things are going on at the Alameda I don't like."

"What things?"

"I found that Alphonso is more dangerous than a rattle-snake. He has me scared."

"I know that, but what's going on at the Alameda?"

"People who talk come to a sudden end."

"Like old Pete."

"And those two kids. I'm not talking. I don't want to end up the way they did."

"Who wants to? But something is going on there, huh?"

"He's hiding people there. He's given them the top floor."

"Who?"

"I don't know, and don't want to know." She set down her coffee cup. "Bart, I want out. I've had it up to here with this goddamn City. It's time I moved on. I want to go to 'Frisco. There's a guy there who does an act, and he wants me to join him, but he needs me to put up some money."

"They always do, baby. Don't get conned again."

"He's different. Will you stake me for ten thousand dollars, Bart?"

I gaped at her.

"I've got buzzing in my ears. For a moment, I imagined you said ten thousand dollars."

She nodded.

"That's what I said."

131

"Ten thousand! Baby! That's insane! I haven't even two thousand."

"Don't lie!" Her face turned vicious. "I know Alphonso shut your mouth with fifty thousand. I was listening outside the door. I want ten of that or else. . . ."

I suddenly realized I hadn't any clothes on. The happy, sexy atmosphere had suddenly vanished. I slid off the bed and went into the bathroom. I shaved and showered, taking my time, my mind busy. When a woman, looking the way Gloria looked and said *or else* I knew I had to handle her very carefully.

When I returned to the bedroom, Gloria was dressed. She stood looking out of the window, her back turned to me, cigarette smoke making a spiral above her carroty hair.

I dressed, then went to the closet for my police special. The holster was hanging on the peg, but the gun was missing.

Bart, baby, I said to myself, you really have to handle this one with extreme care.

Gloria turned and lifted her right hand. The police special pointed at me.

"Looking for this, Bart?" Her voice was harsh and her eyes cold as ice.

"You wouldn't want to shoot me, would you, honey?"

"I'll shoot you in your goddamn leg if you don't give me that money," she said, and she looked vicious enough to do just that.

I moved carefully away and sat down.

"You squeezed fifty thousand out of Alphonso," she went on, "now I'm going to squeeze ten thousand out of you."

I drew in a long uneasy breath.

"Baby, I would give it to you if I had it. I've spent it."

"Don't give me that crap! No one spends that much money in five weeks!"

"You're right. No one does, except me. I have a talent for spending money. I also have a talent for finding expensive dolls. All that beautiful loot went on a four week cruise. Where do you think I got this tan from? Working in a coal mine?"

She stared at me, and I saw her face start to fall to pieces.

"I want a get-away stake!" She lowered the gun. "You can't have spent all that money!" A faint wail of misery crept into her voice. I relaxed a little. I was now over the danger line.

"I did. I can prove it. We'll go to my bank, and they'll tell you."

"Oh, shut up!" She threw the gun on the bed and turned her back on me. I slid out of my chair, whipped up the gun and dropped it into my pocket. I began to breathe normally.

She spun around.

"What am I going to do? Freddie can't have me unless I go into partnership with him. Can't you find some money, Bart?"

"Rest your fanny, baby. Let's see what we can do. Now start using your brains. Have you asked yourself why Diaz parted with fifty thousand without even a whimper."

She sat down and stared at me.

"Why did he?"

"Because I opened such a can of worms he had to pay me to keep quiet."

"What can of worms?"

"That's something you don't want to know about. It's to do with this guy Diaz is hiding."

"You mean the man and the woman?"

"A woman?"

"There's a woman with him. I've heard them talking."

I remembered the two beds in the tent on the pirates' island, and the woman's things I had seen. I had thought Nancy had used them when visiting Pofferi.

"Are you sure there's a woman with him?"

"I'm sure. Who is he? What's the fuss about?"

"Leave it. You want ten thousand to go to 'Frisco . . . right?"

"Are you deaf?" She thumped her fists on her knees. "I told you, didn't I?"

"You could earn it, baby."

She moved uneasily as she stared at me.

"You kidding?"

"You could earn it."

"How?"

"I want to know what goes on at the Alameda. I want to know about this man and this woman Diaz is hiding. I want you to find out about them and tell me."

She reared back.

"Do you imagine I'm that crazy?" Her voice was shrill. "I'm not finishing up like Pete and those two kids. No way!"

"Relax! All you have to do is to bug Diaz's office. I've a gimmick which activates a tape recorder when someone starts talking. All you have to do is to plant the bug. No problem, baby. I'll give you the bug and a recorder. Change the tape when it runs out. In one week from now, I'll pay you ten thousand beautiful dollars in return for the tapes. How's about it?"

I knew I was getting carried away. Unless Hamel came up with a million, I would never find ten thousand, but she wasn't to know that. If the tapes came up with evidence that Diaz killed Pete and the two kids, I could squeeze him dry.

"Where will the ten thousand come from?" Gloria demanded. "You've just said you have no money."

I gave her a confident smile.

"I haven't right now, baby, but in a week, I will have. With some of the money I got from Diaz I bought a share of action with a friend of mine," I lied. "It cost me five, but the return is a certain fifteen. Ten for you: five for me."

I knew she had been conned most of her life by guys who could spin her a yarn. If I had even thought of spinning such a yarn to Bertha she would have crowned me with a beer bottle, but Gloria wasn't in the same league as Bertha.

I watched her think. I could almost hear her think. There was a red light flashing in her tiny mind, warning her not to trust me, but the thought of getting her hands on ten thousand dollars turned the red light to green.

"How do I know you'll give me the money?" she demanded.

"I swear it on my father's tomb."

She studied me suspiciously.

"How do I know your father is dead?"

"For Pete's sake! Dial Heaven: they'll tell you."

She thought some more, but greed won over caution.

"Okay, I'll do it, but if you don't give me the money, I'll cut off your family jewels."

*　　*　　*

Washington Smith joined Jarvis and me for lunch. He had had a telephone call from Hamel, saying he would be returning that evening. It appeared the director of the film had been taken ill, so the meeting had been postponed for a week. Smith would be required to unpack for Hamel.

"How is Mrs. Hamel?" I asked, as Jarvis served chicken Maryland.

"I am glad to say she is much better. She left soon after Mr. Hamel departed. I understand she is spending the day on the yacht. Sun and the sea are great healers."

It was while we were finishing the meal, the sound of a deep throated engine made Smith get to his feet.

"That must be Mrs. Hamel returning," he said. "I know the sound of her car anywhere. I had better go."

"Now, Mr. Smith," Jarvis said, chidingly. "I am sure Mrs. Hamel won't expect you to be on duty at lunch time. I have a very special Stilton I would like you to try."

Smith hesitated, then sat down.

"Yes, you're right. I informed Mrs. Hamel that I would be lunching here. A Stilton? What luxury!"

135

I pushed back my chair.

"I'd better show the flag," I said, "but I won't be long," and winking at Jarvis, I set off down the drive towards the gates.

As soon as I was out of sight of the cottage, I broke into a run and climbed the tree to over-look the opposite hedge.

The Ferrari was standing before the house. The front door stood open. I waited. After five minutes or so, Nancy came out. She was wearing a dark blue turtle neck sweater, white slacks, her hair concealed by a red scarf, and enormous black goggles masked her face. She slid into the car and drove down to the gates which opened automatically. I looked straight down onto the roof of the car as, with a roar, it sped away.

I climbed down the tree and walked back to the cottage. Smith looked inquiringly at me as I took my place at the table.

"She's gone," I said. "She must have forgotten something."

"Yes. Ladies have a habit of forgetting things. I left a note saying Mr. Hamel would be back at seven. No doubt she saw it."

"Try a little more," Jarvis said, scooping a big portion from the napkin wrapped cheese.

Smith left after 15.00. Jarvis retired for a nap. I sat in the shade, and also took a nap.

Around 19.00 while Jarvis was supervising the dinner, I again climbed the tree. There was no sign of the Ferrari. After a few minutes of patient waiting, I saw a taxi pull up. Hamel got out. He paid the cabby, then using a key, he unlocked the gates and walked up the drive. I saw he had swung the gates to, but they didn't close.

As I watched him approach the house, I wondered if he would be surprised that Nancy wasn't there to greet him. I also wondered where she was. She had been away from the house now for over six hours.

I descended the tree and walked back to the cottage.

"Ah, there you are, Mr. Anderson. I was about to call

you," Jarvis said. "I hope this will be to your taste."

I regarded the silver dish on which lay a magnificent salmon, poached in a cream and herb sauce.

"It looks good enough for two honest, hard-working men to eat, Mr. Jarvis," I said, sitting at the table.

"I think champagne goes well with salmon. I ventured to put a bottle in the ice bucket."

Man! I thought. This is the way to live!

As we ate, I launched into one of my fabricated crime stories. It was sometime after 21.00 that I brought the yarn to an exciting conclusion. We were sipping coffee, with a Napoleon brandy for support, when we both heard the sharp bang of a fired gun.

I put down my coffee cup and jumped to my feet. The shot had come from across the road.

Leaving Jarvis gaping, I ran fast down the drive to the gates. I was sure the shot had come from Hamel's place. Moving across the road, I shoved open the Hamel gates, and started up the drive to the ranch house.

As I reached the front door, it was open, and Washington Smith appeared in the doorway. He was shaking, his eyes rolling, his face the colour of lead.

"Oh, Mr. Anderson . . ."

"Take it easy," I said, and caught hold of him.

"Mr. Hamel . . . in his study," Smith gasped, then his knees buckled.

I pushed him aside and walked into the big lobby. A fat, elderly negress sat on a chair, her apron covering her face, and she was making whimpering sounds. Crossing the patio, I walked to Hamel's study. The door stood wide open.

I smelt gun smoke. Pausing, I looked into the big room where, not so long ago, Hamel had talked to me.

Facing me was his big desk. He sat behind the desk, his head resting on the highback of the desk chair, his eyes staring at me with the emptiness of death. Blood trickled down the right side of his face. Powder burns discoloured the small hole in his temple.

For a long moment, I stood looking at him and the only thought that came to me was I would now never own a million dollars. Then shaking off this depression, I moved into the room, and up to the desk. On the floor, by the chair lay a Beretta 6.35 pistol. I looked at it, but didn't touch it. The air conditioner was on. The windows were closed. My eyes travelled to the desk. An IBM typewriter stood before Hamel and there was a sheet of paper in the machine.

There was writing. I leaned forward and read:

Why go on? I am of no use to a woman. I have spoilt two marriages. Why go on?

I stood away and stared at the dead man.

"You poor sap," I said, half aloud. "You certainly got your values wrong."

"Mr. Anderson . . ."

I turned.

Smith stood wringing his hands, in the doorway.

"He's dead," I said. "Don't touch anything here." I moved out of the room and closed the door. "Where's Mrs. Hamel?"

"Dead? Oh, Mr. Anderson . . . he was so good to us."

"Get hold of yourself!" I barked. "Where's Mrs. Hamel?"

"I don't know. She hasn't returned."

Then it flashed into my mind that if Nancy found me — the guy who had bitten her for fifty thousand dollars — plus the news her husband had killed himself, she might flip and start trouble I wouldn't want. I decided to do a quick fade.

"Mr. Smith! Listen carefully. I'll get action. Don't let Mrs. Hamel go in there. Just wait . . . okay?"

He nodded dumbly.

Moving fast, I left the ranch house and ran back to the cottage where Jarvis was waiting, his big black eyes alarmed question marks.

Briefly, I told him that Hamel had killed himself. Then I went into the cottage for the telephone, then paused. Mel

Palmer had to be the first on the scene, then the cops.

Jarvis was hovering around.

"Got a telephone book?" I demanded.

He produced the local book. I found Palmer's home number and, praying he would be home, I dialled.

I had to talk my way around a snooty sounding butler before Palmer came on the line.

"What is it, Mr. Anderson?" he asked crossly. "I have guests."

"Russ Hamel has just shot himself," I said. "He's dead. Mrs. Hamel isn't home. There's a suicide note in his typewriter the press will love. I leave it to you to call the police."

"I don't believe it!" Palmer croaked.

"He's dead. Get moving," and I hung up.

As I moved out of the cottage into the humid darkness, I heard the throaty roar of the Ferrari. Nancy was back! I belted down the drive and climbed the tree. I was in time to see Nancy getting out of the car. She walked slowly up the steps to the front door. The porch light was on and I could see her clearly. Then Smith opened the door. He stepped back, and she moved forward and out of sight. The door closed.

I would have given a lot to have been able to watch Nancy's reactions when Smith broke the news to her. Had she loved Hamel or had she married him only to escape from the Italian police?

Then a thought struck me with considerable force. By Hamel's stupid suicide, Nancy would inherit his wealth, his copyrights and his film earnings. As his widow, she would become immensely rich!

Then my mind switched to Pofferi. According to Lu Coldwell, Pofferi had come to the United States to raise money for his murderous organisation. Nancy was his wife. He would have access to Hamel's fortune to be used to finance the Red Brigade!

I climbed down the tree and walked back to the cottage, my mind busy. As I reached the cottage, I heard the telephone bell ringing. Entering, I picked up the receiver.

"Mr. Anderson," Jarvis said. "Mr. Herschenheimer heard the shot. He is extremely nervous. I am staying with him. Will you watch the gates? I told him about this unfortunate suicide, but he doesn't believe it. He is sure an assassin is on the island."

"Okay," I said. "Tell him no one will get near him."

"Thank you, Mr. Anderson. He will be relieved."

I replaced the receiver, then realizing that Mel Palmer could have trouble getting past the security barrier, I called Mike O'Flagherty at the guardhouse.

I explained the situation.

"I've alerted Mr. Hamel's agent, Mr. Palmer," I said. "He'll be arriving any moment. Let him through, Mike. The police will also be arriving. Let them through."

"Holy Mary!" Mike exclaimed. "The poor man has killed himself?"

"Let Mr. Palmer through," I said, and hung up.

I went down to the gates and waited. Ten minutes later, a Cadillac pulled up outside Hamel's gates. I watched Palmer get out of the car, push open the gates and hurry up the drive.

I waited, and while I waited, I thought of the fifty thousand dollars I had squandered. I stopped thinking when I began to think of my future: those thoughts were too depressing.

Around 23.00, a police car arrived. From it spilled Tom Lepski and Max Jacoby. I walked across the road as they got from the car.

Lepski regarded me.

"What's cooking?" he demanded.

I explained I had been on duty guarding Herschenheimer. I had heard a shot, found Hamel dead, alerted Palmer and was now back on guard duty.

Lepski glared at me.

"Why didn't you call us?"

"That's Palmer's job," I said. "The suicide note could

be damaging. There's a load of money involved."

"What suicide note?"

"Hamel was impotent according to the note. The press will love it, Tom. A big selling author of porno, impotent! It's something only Palmer can handle."

"You have been up there?"

"I found him."

Lepski's eyes narrowed.

"Touch anything?"

"Come on, Tom, you know better than to ask a stupid question. Mrs. Hamel was out on the yacht. She got back around half an hour ago."

"Okay. I'll want to talk to you again," and he and Jacoby hurried up the drive.

Just before midnight, Carl arrived to relieve me.

"Mike told me," he said. "Excitements, huh?"

"You can say that. The old nut is laying an egg. He heard the shot."

Carl groaned.

"That means I keep awake tonight."

"That's what it means."

"Had some excitement down on the waterfront this afternoon," he said, and laughed. "Some joker let off a smoke bomb on the harbour. Man! You should have seen the panic! I was getting a snack at the Alameda bar when the bomb went off. In two seconds, the rubber-neckers and all the other crumbs vanished. Some kid, I guess, but you should have seen how fast everyone ran."

I wasn't interested.

"I guess I'll get home," I said. "See you tomorrow and keep alert."

Carl laughed.

"Oh, sure."

"If the cops want me, tell them I'm home."

"Why should they want you?"

"Why do cops want anything?"

We walked together up the drive.

"Why did this rich jerk want to knock himself off?"

141

"It happens," I said, started the car and drove down to the barrier.

O'Flaherty came out of the guardhouse.

"What a thing!" he said. "Why should Mr. Hamel do that?"

"It happens," I said and gunned the engine impatiently. He took the hint and lifted the pole. I gave him a wave and headed for home.

The first thing I did when I had shut my front door was to pour a double Scotch. I took the drink to a lounging chair and sat down.

The time was 00.30. Should I call Bertha and break the news? I didn't believe she had sold her apartment and her furniture, but suppose she had? I had a depressing feeling that as soon as she learned there was to be no million dollars, I would see the last of her.

The telephone bell rang.

Bertha?

I hesitated, then got up and walked over to the desk. Lifting the receiver, I said, "Hello there?"

"Mr. Anderson?"

I stiffened. I recognized Joey's voice.

"That you, Joey?"

"Yes, Mr. Anderson."

"I've been trying to contact you. I wanted to tell you how sorry I am about Jimbo. Where are you calling from?"

"Mr. Anderson, that man left the Alameda this morning. I've been trying to get you."

"The man who's hiding there?"

"Yes, Mr. Anderson. I saw him leave. I saw someone throw something from the upper window. It exploded in smoke. There was excitement. While everyone was running, the bearded man came out and got in the boot of a car that was parked right outside."

"What car, Joey?"

"A Ferrari. There was a woman, driving. As soon as he was in the trunk, she drove off. No one saw, but me.

142

Everyone was running around because of the smoke."

"What time was this, Joey?"

"Eleven forty, Mr. Anderson."

"Was the woman wearing a red head scarf and big sunglasses?"

"Yes, Mr. Anderson."

"Right. Now listen, Joey . . ."

The line went dead as he hung up.

I replaced the receiver and stood staring down at the carpet.

Nancy had left home soon after Hamel had left for Hollywood. She had returned a little after midday and had left again five minutes later.

I lit a cigarette with a slightly unsteady hand.

She had brought Pofferi, hidden in the trunk of the Ferrari, to the ranch house. O'Flagherty would have waved her through.

Pofferi had been hidden somewhere in the ranch house when Hamel had returned.

Suicide?

I crushed out my cigarette.

Hamel hadn't committed suicide. Pofferi had murdered him!

143

CHAPTER EIGHT

As I sat thinking, the pieces of the jig-saw began to fall into place.

Hamel, enormously rich, had met Nancy (Lucia Pofferi) in Rome, and had fallen for her. He wasn't to know that she was on the run for two murders. By dying her hair dark and wearing big sun goggles, she had evaded the police hunt, but she knew the net was drawing tighter. Hamel had offered marriage. The fact that she was already married to Pofferi didn't stop her accepting. By marrying Hamel she had the safe way of escaping from Italy.

Pofferi, also hunted by the police, had been trying to raise funds for his murderous organisation. Nancy would inherit Hamel's fortune if she became Hamel's widow. Once she got the money, Pofferi would use it for his organisation. Somehow, Pofferi had reached the United States, and with Nancy's help, had hidden on the pirates' island. He had learned from Nancy that Hamel was impotent.

The pair had been patient. They had waited some six weeks before putting their plan into operation. They wanted Hamel to finish his book and collect all those millions on the advances. As soon as he had finished the book, they moved into action.

Nancy knew she couldn't get Pofferi past the barrier without O'Flagherty spotting him. Probably Pofferi had solved this problem by creating a diversion on the waterfront, hiding in the trunk of the Ferrari, and O'Flagherty had been fooled.

When the police investigated Hamel's death, they would be satisfied that no outsider could have been involved. Nancy was out on the yacht. Washington Smith and his wife were above suspicion. So . . . suicide.

But I knew Nancy had smuggled Pofferi into the ranch house, and I was now certain Pofferi had shot Hamel and had staged the scene to look like suicide.

I sat up with a jerk.

Right at this moment, Pofferi must be hiding somewhere in the ranch house. He couldn't get off the Largo without Nancy's help, and she had to stay to answer police questions.

So what should I do? Call the cops and tell them that Pofferi was hiding in the ranch house? Then what?

Keep out of it, baby, I said to myself. If you start flapping with your mouth, you'll be in trouble. So keep out of it.

I went to bed. It took me a little time before I slept. For the first ten minutes, I wondered what Pofferi was doing: what Nancy was doing: what the cops were doing. I had no answers, so eventually, I slept.

The telephone bell woke me at 10.23. I dragged myself across the bed and picked up the receiver.

"Yeah?"

"Bart!" Bertha's strident voice slammed against my eardrum.

"Hi, honey," I said feebly.

"Have you seen the papers? Hamel's shot himself!"

"Yeah . . . I know."

"Did you talk to him?"

"For God's sake, baby . . ."

"Did you talk to him?"

"No."

She made a noise like a hornet trapped in a bottle.

"Okay, Bart. You have had your chance, and you fluffed it."

"You can say that again."

"My Fink called me. He wants to marry me."

I stiffened.

"Do you want to marry him, baby?"

"Why not? He has this yacht, a penthouse, servants

145

and a bloated bank account, so why not?"

"Wait a minute! Think! Do you want to spend the next best years of your life waving your fanny at a kink?"

"For that yacht, his penthouse, his slaves and his money, I'd do a lot more than wave my ass. Wouldn't you?"

I heaved a sigh.

"You have a point. Okay, go ahead and marry him. Be happy."

"When I marry him, I'll be faithful. This is the big goodbye, Bart. You can't say you didn't have your chance," and she hung up.

I lay back on the pillow, feeling depressed, then I began to use my smart brain. There were many other beautiful dolls in the world. Variety is the spice of life, and a change of doll-scene offered fresh excitement. Anyway, that gag about Bertha being faithful, was the big laugh of the day.

I went asleep again.

*　　　*　　　*

After a late dinner, I read Hamel's obituary in *The Paradise City Herald*. His suicide made front page headlines. There was no mention of the suicide note. I guessed Mel Palmer had swept that under the rug. There was a vague suggestion that Hamel had been over-working and had become depressed. His wife had collapsed, and Palmer, very much in charge, had gone down to the barrier to be interviewed by the press and the T.V. vultures. No one was allowed past the barrier. I imagined Mike O'Flagherty was having the time of his life. Palmer had made a brief statement. Mrs. Hamel would grant no interviews.

All around me in the restaurant, people were talking about Hamel's death.

One loud-mouthed woman summed it up. She said, "Well, when a guy writes the muck he did, he must have been a nut-case. I mean, those bedroom scenes! He's better off dead."

I wanted to tell her how wrong she was, but I didn't. I thought of Hamel. I had liked him. I felt sorry for him.

Soon after 23.20, I drove to Paradise Largo. As I pulled up at the barrier, I saw some dozen men, sitting on the grass verge, smoking and talking. The press vultures never gave up!

O'Flagherty came out of the guardhouse.

"Man!" I said. "You are certainly having a ball!"

He grinned.

"Yeah. No one gets by me, Bart. No one got by me. I told Lepski." O'Flagherty's moon-shaped face was glistening with sweat. "What a thing!"

"Sure is." I waited until he raised the pole, watched by envious eyes, then I drove to Herschenheimer's gates. Carl let me in.

"Man!" he exclaimed. "The old man's flipping."

"So?"

He grinned.

"So nothing. He's keeping Jarvis out of bed. Just look busy. I've had enough of it. See you."

When he had gone, I went into the cottage, found a pack of sandwiches waiting, and I sat down. I wondered what was going on across the road. I wondered if Palmer was still there, fussing around.

As I began to eat the sandwiches, Jarvis appeared. I saw he was doing a flipping act.

"Mr. Anderson, I couldn't sleep until I talked to you."

"Something wrong?"

"Yes." He moved forward and sat down. "What a day I've had! I have had to give Mr. Herschenheimer a sedative. He is now sleeping."

I munched on the third sandwich.

"What's cooking?"

"Mr. Washington Smith and his wife have been dismissed."

This news didn't surprise me. It made sense. Knowing

what I knew, Smith and his wife would be a menace to Pofferi, hiding in the house.

I put on my surprised expression.

"Dismissed?"

"Yes." Jarvis looked miserable. "Mr. Palmer told them they must go immediately. They were given no time . . . just pack and go. Dreadful! After fifteen years of faithful service! They were paid a year's salary. Mr. Palmer explained that Mrs. Hamel wanted them to go. He was nice about it. He seemed shocked."

"That's tough," I said.

"I will miss Mr. Smith. It is difficult to understand. Mr. and Mrs. Smith kept that house beautifully."

"Any news of Mrs. Hamel?"

Jarvis lifted his lean shoulders. From his expression, I could see Nancy Hamel was no longer in favour.

"Mr. Smith didn't even see her to say goodbye. It was so abrupt."

I took another sandwich: thinly cut lobster meat with a touch of mayonaise.

"So who's going to run the house?"

"That is something Mr. Smith or I cannot understand. Mr. Smith was told by Mr. Palmer that Josh Jones will look after things until Mrs. Hamel leaves. She intends to sell the estate as soon as the burial has taken place."

"Josh Jones? Who is he?" I asked, probing.

"Mr. Hamel's crewman." Jarvis looked down his nose. "A no-good nigger."

"Is Mr. Palmer still over there?"

"He left after the police had gone."

I now had all the information I needed. I wanted Jarvis out of the way. I told him he looked tired. I said I would be right here if he needed me and taking the hint, he went back to the house. I gave him five minutes, then walked down to the gates and climbed the tree.

There was a light on in the living room, but the curtains were drawn. I wondered if Nancy and Pofferi were behind those curtains, talking together, planning what they would do with the money once Nancy inherited it. I sat with my back against the tree, waiting and watching.

Nothing happened.

After an hour, the light went out and a light went on in a room at the far end of the ranch house. Nancy's bedroom? Then I heard the sound of a car approaching. Leaning forward, I saw the car stop outside Hamel's gates. From my perch in the tree, I could see right down on the car's roof. I watched Josh Jones get out of the car, thumb the red button and wait. The gates opened. He slid into the car and drove up the drive. The gates automatically closed.

The porch light went on as he pulled up and the front door opened.

Framed in the doorway was Pofferi!

There was no mistaking the broad shouldered, squat figure. Jones shouted to him and the porch light went out. I tried to pierce the darkness, but I could only make out the silhouette of the car.

Then the lights went on behind the curtains of the living room.

Resting my back against the trunk of the tree, I waited. After some minutes, another light went on in the room next to Nancy's room. I waited. Time crawled by, then all the lights went out.

I slid down the tree and returned to the cottage. Jarvis had left a bottle of Scotch on the desk. I poured, drank and sat down.

Then a beautiful idea struck me. There were times when even I surprised myself when my money hunting mind clicks into action.

A million dollars!

Bart, baby, I said to myself, it's waiting for you across the road. Play your cards right, and you have it made.

Across the road, in Hamel's house, two terrorists were hiding. One of them would inherit Hamel's fortune. I had no idea what he was worth, but the fact this book would bring in eleven million gross, he must be worth at least twenty million.

Twenty million! And I had been dim enough to wonder why Diaz had parted with fifty thousand without a whimper to keep me quiet. Man! Had I been dim! Diaz knew that if I had blown the whistle, some twenty million or more would have gone down the drain. No wonder he parted so easily. Fifty thousand . . . peanuts!

I thought of Diaz.

I promise you one thing, if you try to put pressure on me again, you will have an unpleasant end.

Oh, yeah?

That cheap grease-ball wasn't going to scare me away from a million dollars.

There was a typewriter on the desk.

More paper work, Bart, baby, I said. More life insurance. I typed out in duplicate, the facts as I knew them: how Nancy had smuggled Pofferi into the ranch house, how she had gone off in the yacht to establish an alibi, how Pofferi had murdered Hamel to look like suicide, and that he and Nancy were still in the ranch house, bottled up by the waiting press.

I put the original of the statement in an envelope which I addressed to Howard Selby with a covering note. If he didn't hear from me within twenty-four hours, he was to hand the envelope to Chief of Police Terrell. The second copy I put in another envelope.

I made myself a drink and relaxed back in a lounging chair. I thought out the next moves.

Later, when I was satisfied I had got the scene set, I turned my mind to what I would do with a million dollars.

I wondered if I should telephone Bertha and tell her not to marry her Fink. Bertha had become a habit with me. I hesitated about losing her. I thought some more and decided to hell with her! It would be fun to sit back and let the dolly birds chase me for a change. Would they come arunning, once the news leaked out that I was worth a million!

Dreams!

* * *

As soon as Carl relieved me at midday the following morning, I got in the Maser and drove to the Trueman building. There I handed my statement to the mousy looking girl, telling her I wanted a receipt. I stood over her while she typed to my dictation on Selby's letter heading. I waited until she took the receipt into Selby who had a client. She returned with his signature and I told her to lock the letter in the safe.

Bug-eyed, she said she would.

Just to give her a thrill, I gave her my sexy smile, and said in my alluring voice, "You have beautiful hands."

There was nothing else about her I could say truthfully. She turned the colour of a cooked beetroot and simpered.

I left, knowing that I had made her day.

The Parnell Agency had many informers on the payroll. It cost the Colonel a bomb, but then he was loaded with the green, and to have ears to the ground was essential to the successful running of his business.

I contacted Amelia Bronson who was Mark Highbee's second secretary.

Amelia Bronson was a fat, middle aged harridan, with a face like a discarded boot, but with a brain that would make a razor blade seem blunt. She had been on the Agency's gift-roll for some time. She got a turkey and two bottles of Scotch each Christmas, and a hamper of food on her birthday. So far, the Agency hadn't asked for a *quid pro quo*.

I took her to an Italian restaurant where she demolished an enormous plate of spaghetti, four vast pieces of *Osso Bucco*, plus cheese, plus a banana split. Coffee and brandy left her placid and ready to talk.

Mark Highbee was Russ Hamel's attorney. He would be handling Hamel's affairs. Amelia would be doing the paper work. So I asked questions, and Amelia, bloated with food, answered them.

I slid her a hundred dollar bill when we parted. I

hated to do this, but Amelia liked money as much as she liked food.

I then drove to Solly Finklestein's office. I had a little trouble getting to see him. S.F. (as he was known in the City) was absorbed in making money. He was the biggest loan shark on the Pacific Coast. Here again, he got a hamper of luxury food every Christmas from the Agency, and when we needed information about who was borrowing, who was in the squeeze, S.F. parted with the necessary.

I talked to him about raising a loan for a million. He said there was nothing difficult about that. It was some cheapie who wanted to raise a hundred thousand that caus~d trouble. But for a million, his rates were 25 %, and the collateral wasn't all that important. He grinned his shark's grin.

"We collect on bad payers, Bart."

I knew what that meant. Some thug would arrive with a length of lead piping. You paid or else.

By this time, I had all the necessary ammunition. Feeling confident, I drove down to the waterfront. I sat in the Maser and surveyed the scene. Tourists jostled, the vendors shouted big discounts, fishing boats were unloading.

I thought of Diaz.

A dangerous snake, but I felt confident I had him in such a squeeze, he wouldn't strike back.

I fingered the gun in the holster under my jacket. Then bracing myself, I got out of the car and walked to the Alameda bar.

The fat Mexican barkeep gave me an oily grin as I walked up to the crowded bar. The riff-raff and the fishermen stared at me, then returned to their drinks.

"Diaz," I said to the barkeep.

He nodded, went down the bar to the telephone and as he began to talk, I walked along the bar and through to Diaz's office. I pushed open the door and paused. Diaz was behind his desk, a cigar clamped between his teeth. He was putting down the telephone receiver as I walked in.

"Hi!" I said. "Remember me?"

I shoved an upright chair close to his desk and strided it, giving him my friendly smile.

"I thought I told you to stay clear of me," he said softly. His voice was like the hissing of a snake.

"Times change," I said. "Yesterday isn't today."

He tapped ash off his cigar onto the floor. His snake-like face was expressionless.

"What do you want?"

"You have yourself a new partner," I said. "Me."

"I warned you, you sonofabitch. So okay, this is where you get yours," Diaz snarled, and a gun jumped into his hand.

I continued to smile at him.

"You have enough intelligence not to shoot me in your office," I said. "You have enough intelligence not to shoot me anywhere. You have a new partner. There's nothing you can do about it unless, of course, you want to lose more than twenty million dollars, and that I can't believe."

His eyes wavered and he lowered the gun.

"Listen, you blackmailing creep . . ." he began, then stopped.

A cheap bluffer, I told myself. This was going to be easy.

"Let me spell it out," I said. "It's nothing you don't know, but I want you to know I know. I guess Pofferi dreamed up the idea. I don't imagine you did. You climbed on the gravy train as I am doing. As I see it, when Pofferi found out that Hamel, worth millions, had fallen for his wife, he saw his chance of cashing in. Nancy was on the run from the Italian cops with two murders tucked up her jersey. When Hamel offered marriage, Pofferi saw that Nancy could get out of Italy and she would inherit Hamel's loot if and when he died. So Nancy married Hamel and Pofferi managed to get here. He hid up on an island. Nancy took care of him. Then I arrived on the

153

scene, and, in a panic, Pofferi, through Josh Jones, came to you. You made a deal with him in return for protection. When I put the squeeze to Nancy, she alerted you. You, acting as her agent, decided to pay me off. You did a great job. You had me fooled. That psychological gimmick of yours to produce fifty grand in cash bought me off. It bought me off until I found out just how big the take was, and that Pofferi, aided by Nancy, had murdered Hamel, faking suicide." I took from my wallet the statement I had written and dropped it in front of him. I added Selby's receipt. "Take a look," I went on. "It's all in print."

I saw sweat begin to trickle down his face as he read the statement and examined the receipt.

"So, go ahead and shoot me," I said, smiling at him. "If you do, away goes all that lovely green and you and your buddies go behind bars for life. But don't let that stop you . . . go ahead and shoot."

He put down the gun, then stared at me, his snake-like eyes glazed.

"I'm not being greedy," I said. "All I want is one million dollars, and I want it right now. I could squeeze you for a lot more, but a million will be fine. You and your buddies will still have lots of millions left. I can't be fairer than that, can I?"

He just sat there, staring at me.

"I have information for you," I went on, enjoying myself. "First, it will take three months to wind up Hamel's estate. The good news is Nancy inherits the lot. Could be around twenty millions. There will be a big yearly income from the copyrights, and this could go on for some years. The pay-off is nice, huh?"

Still he sat there saying nothing.

"I want an immediate million." I leaned forward, and gave him my friendly smile. "That is no problem. I have talked with Solly Finklestein. On your signature, he will loan you a million at twenty-five per cent. He will want your joint as collateral: just good will, you understand. If, of course, you don't repay, he will send his boys around but with all those millions coming, that's no problem for you. Are you following me?"

He began to look like a snake cornered by a mongoose.

"All you have to do is to sign this paper Solly has drawn up, and we are in business." I took from my wallet the contract S.F. had dictated and put it before Diaz.

"I'm not signing anything," he mumbled, but he leaned forward and read the contract. "I'm not signing this!" he squealed. "Do you think I'm crazy?"

"You would be crazy not to sign it, partner," I said. "If you don't: bye-bye millions. Twenty years behind bars. It's up to you."

He sat there, sweat oozing out of his face, as he stared at the contract. Solly Finklestein was well known and what was more important, his methods of collecting bad debts were better known. Diaz knew if he signed, then couldn't pay, he would be crippled for the rest of his days.

"Wake up, stupe!" I said, losing patience with him. "Sign now or I'll blow the whistle. I could get off with a three-year stretch, but you and your buddies lose millions and gain a twenty-year stretch. Make up your tiny mind!"

He moved: nothing more lethal than wiping the sweat off his face.

"Relax, partner," I said to encourage him. "You won't see me again. As soon as Solly gives me the loot, I'm shaking the dust off this City. Think what you and your buddies can do with all those millions, plus a big income for years."

I knew I had him in such a squeeze, there could be no blow back, and there wasn't. With an unsteady hand, he picked up a pen.

I watched him.

A million dollars.

I could hear the patter of feet as the dolls came chasing.

Then the scene turned sour. I saw Diaz stiffen and stare beyond me. I say his face start to fall to pieces.

A kid's voice said shrilly, "You killed my brothers, senor Diaz. Now, I kill you."

I jerked around.

Joey was standing in the doorway. In his small, dirty hand, he held a .38 revolver. It was pointing at Diaz.

"No, Joey!" I yelled.

The bang of the gun shook the room.

My eyes shifted to Diaz. His face had exploded in a mess of blood. He sat there, the pen in his hand, the contract unsigned.

I moved fast. Jumping to my feet, I snatched up the contract, my statement and Selby's receipt. I stuffed the papers in my pocket, then I spun around.

Joey smiled at me. It was the happy smile of a child who has been given a gift-wrapped parcel.

"No one kills my people, Mr. Anderson," he said. "They die too."

"Get the hell out of here!" I shouted at him.

"Yes, Mr. Anderson." He smiled again and walked out of the room.

He didn't get far. Three big Mexicans grabbed him and hustled him back into the office. One of them had snatched the gun from him.

The office became crowded. Three hustlers, who had pushed their way in, began to scream. Everyone was staring at what was left of Diaz.

I slid around them to the door.

Above the uproar, I heard Joey's treble voice shouting in triumph: "I killed him! I killed him! Do you hear me, Tommy? Do you hear me Jimbo? I killed him!"

I fought my way out onto the street, slid into the Maser, and was driving away, as the cop sirens began to cut the air.

*   *   *

By the time I got back to my apartment, I was in a state of depression, and in a cold sweat of fear.

My foremost thought was whether the cops would get onto me.

As I paced the big living room, I told myself that no one at the Alameda knew me by name. The barkeep knew I had seen Diaz twice, and he knew I had been in Diaz's office when Joey pulled the trigger. In the confusion, I had slid away. I was sure no-one noticed me leaving, but would the cops start asking questions? Joey was caught. It should be an open-and-shut case, but when the cops started questioning him, would he pull me into the mess?

Take it easy, baby, I said to myself. You were a good pal of Joey. He won't give you away.

I poured myself a drink, tossed it back, then refilled the glass.

You hope, baby, he won't give you away, I thought. There's nothing you can do about it, but hope.

What now?

Diaz was dead, but Nancy and Pofferi were very much alive. I thought of those two, with Josh Jones, hiding in Hamel's house: three deadly, dangerous people. As much as I liked picking up a million dollars, I was not going to put the squeeze on them. It would be like fooling with nitroglycerin.

Bart, baby, I said to myself, kiss that million goodbye. Those three are out of your league. All you can now hope for is you don't get the cops on your neck. If you have any luck, you won't. Then you return to the Agency, and you go on working for peanuts, and you look around for some doll who won't be too expensive, and you'll go on and on until the Colonel decides to retire you, and you will settle down on the State and wait for death.

I poured myself another drink.

Man! Was I depressed!

I sat there, thinking of nothing, drinking and getting high. The shadows began to creep across the carpet. In another six hours I would have to report for duty to guard an old nut.

Then the telephone bell rang. I poured another drink and let the bell ring.

Maybe Bertha had changed her mind. I didn't want to

be bothered with Bertha right now. She was the original pain in the ass. So let her ring.

After a while, the telephone bell slumped into silence. In spite of my depression, I felt hungry. I weaved my way into the kitchen. I found nothing in the refrigerator except a bottle of Scotch.

I went back to my chair, sat down and closed my eyes. Time passed. I dreamed I was sitting in the Maser, waiting for an unfaithful wife to come out of a sleazy motel where she had been having it off with a Romeo: my future.

Then the front door bell rang, ringing persistently. I came awake with a jerk.

The cops?

I got to my feet. The short sleep had sobered me. I looked at my watch. The time was 23.05.

The bell rang again.

I smoothed down my hair, straightened my crumpled jacket and went into the lobby. My heart was thumping. My brain revolved around possible lies when Lepski began to shoot questions at me.

The bell rang again.

I opened up.

Gloria Cort pushed by me and walked into the living room.

It only needed this, I thought. She's after the ten thousand I promised her.

With dragging feet, I followed her into the living room.

"Now listen, baby . . ." I began.

"Shut your mouth!" she snapped. "You listen to me!" She dropped onto the settee and regarded me with that expression some women can paste on their faces that set up the red light in any man's mind.

"Have a drink?" I suggested.

"Listen! I'm quitting, but you need to know something before I go."

She looked so tense, I left off reaching for the bottle and slumped into the nearest lounging chair.

"So, okay, I'm listening," I said.

"That bug you gave me. I fixed it, as you said, in Alphonse's office. I listened in. If it hadn't been for that bug, I wouldn't be here. I would have been fished out of the harbour with my brains on my face."

I gaped at her.

"Now, look . . ."

"Listen! That sonofabitch Alphonso was planning to murder me! I listened to him telling that nigger to knock me on the head and toss me into the harbour!" She suddenly smiled. It was a smile a cobra might envy. "I beat him to it. He's dead: I'm alive."

I continued to gape at her.

"By giving me that bug, you saved my life, and you can save Nancy Hamel's life too."

"What the hell are you talking about? Nancy's life?"

"For two nights I have been listening to Pofferi and Diaz talking. Here's something I've only just found out: Nancy has a twin sister. They are identical twins. Nancy and Lucia. Get it?"

The last piece of this jig-saw puzzle dropped into place. The two beds in the tent: the woman I saw leave the yacht with Pofferi and Jones. Lucia, not Nancy!

I was now alert and very sober.

"Keep talking," I said.

"I heard them telling each other how clever they had been. Because Lucia was to replace Nancy, they got rid of Penny Highbee who would have spotted Lucia posing as Nancy. Then Lucia telephoned Nancy, asking her to come to the Alameda. Nancy would do anything for her sister. It was Nancy who financed the escape from Italy and hid those two on the island. When Nancy came, they locked her in a room. Lucia put on Nancy's clothes and drove Pofferi, hidden in the trunk of Nancy's car, to Hamel's place. She had no trouble passing the barrier. The guard thought she was Nancy. Then leaving Pofferi in the house, she took off in the yacht with Jones to establish an alibi. When Pofferi murdered Hamel, Lucia returned. That old goat, Palmer thought she was Nancy. He handled the Fuzz and the press. Last night, Jones took Nancy to Hamel's place. She was drugged. She, Lucia, Pofferi and Jones are still there."

"Jones took her in the trunk of his car?"

She nodded.

That made sense. Lucia, posing as Nancy, must have alerted O'Flagherty by telephone that Jones was coming. There would be no problem at the barrier.

"Nancy and Lucia are identical twins?" I asked.

She made an impatient movement.

"They are like two peas in a pod. I caught a glimpse of Lucia. I wouldn't have known the difference. Now, I'll tell you something else. I heard Alphonso talking to that nigger about me. He said I could make trouble. As Russ's ex. I would want a share when they got their hands on Russ's money. He told Jones to get rid of me: knock me on my head and dump me in the sea. My dear, sweet, boy-friend! Can you imagine?" She smiled, an icy, vicious smile. "So I fixed Alphonso before he fixed me."

I stared at her.

"What's that mean?"

"I knew Alphonso had had those two Indian kids murdered. So I found Joey and gave him one of Alphonso's guns. All Joey wanted was a gun." Again she smiled. "That kid did a real fixing job."

"Jesus!" I said.

"Now, I'm leaving for 'Frisco. I have always known where that snake Alphonso kept his smuggling cash. I have it. I haven't a care in the world."

I pointed like a gun dog.

"How much did you get?"

"Plenty." She gave a hard laugh. "That's not your business. I've come here because those jerks are going to murder Nancy after she has been forced to sign a batch of cheques. They haven't the know-how to forge her signature. When they have the signed cheques, she goes into the sea."

I was scarcely listening. I was wondering how

much loot she had filched from Diaz.

"Baby, I have a great idea," I said, giving her my sexy smile. "How about us going away together? What's wrong with us setting up a beautiful partnership?"

She gave me a look that would curdle milk.

"Did you hear what I said? They will kill that ninny as soon as they have forced her to sign a batch of cheques! Do you want her death on your conscience?"

"Look, baby, how much loot did you get from Diaz?"

She swept out of the chair.

"Is that all you can think about — money?"

I blinked at her.

"What else is there to think about except a doll like you?"

"If I didn't want to tangle with the Fuzz, I'd tell them myself. You won't sleep with yourself if you let them kill that girl!"

"I don't want to sleep with myself! I want to sleep with you, baby. How much did you get?"

She glared at me.

"I thought I had seen every creep in the world, but you take the Oscar."

She stamped out, slamming the door.

I blew out my cheeks, then lit a cigarette. I listened to her car roar away.

Baby, I said to myself, you just can't win. I sat for a while, being sorry for myself, then my mind switched to Nancy.

If you let them kill that girl.

Well, okay, I would have to do something, but I was not going to the cops. Then I thought of Lu Coldwell. He could handle this and keep me covered. The FBI always protected their informers.

I hunted up Coldwell's home number and dialled. After a wait, Coldwell came on the line.

"Lu, this is Bart Anderson," I said. "Come to my place, pronto! It's an emergency."

"For God's sake!" Coldwell said crossly. "I was going to bed. What's so urgent?"

"Not over the phone, Lu. Get your ass over here fast! It's to do with an Italian," and I hung up.

I looked at my watch. The time was 23.45. I called the Herschenheimer house. Carl answered.

"This is Bart," I said. "I'll be late: maybe an hour. Stick around until I arrive with a bottle of Scotch," and I hung up before he began to squeal.

It took Coldwell twenty minutes to come ringing on my doorbell. I let him in.

"What's all this?" he demanded.

I told him the information I was about to give him came from an informer. Before I talked, I wanted his guarantee I was kept under cover.

"I could lose my job, Lu. I came on this thing when I should have been working for the Agency. If you don't give me your word to keep me covered, I'm not talking."

"Pofferi?"

"Yes. I know where he is right now, but no cover, no talk."

"You're covered. Where is he?"

I waved him to a chair, then sitting down myself, I told him the story. I was careful to keep myself out of it, saying my informer had been the guy who had discovered Pofferi on the island. Watching Coldwell, as I talked, I could see he didn't believe me, but he had said he would cover me, and when Coldwell said anything like that, I could rely on him.

When I had finished, he sat back and stared at me.

"You are sure about this?"

"I'm sure. Pofferi and his wife, Lucia, are in Hamel's house right now. They have Nancy there. When the estate is settled, they will force Nancy to sign a batch of cheques, then they will murder her. They will then bleed the estate white and take off. They have Hamel's yacht. It's not far to Cuba. From there, they will move the money to Italy."

He thought for some moments, then he nodded.

"I'll get it organized. Don't worry. I'll keep you under cover. I'll talk to Terrell. I'll need some of his men to stake out the house until we are ready to move in."

"You have all the time in the world," I said. "They'll stay still until the estate is settled. They couldn't have a safer hideout."

"Yeah. We'll move in tomorrow."

"Watch it, Lu. Those three are dangerous. You'll have a shoot out."

He grinned wolfishly.

"That'll save the expense of a trial."

When he had gone, I went down to the garage and got into the Maser.

As I drove fast to Paradise Largo, I thought of Nancy Hamel. A bright idea came into my fertile mind. When she was free and inherited all those lovely millions, I could go to her, explain how I had saved her life, give her my respectful smile and hint she should reward me.

That, I thought, was the least she could do.

CHAPTER NINE

I sat up in the tree and looked down at the ranch house. There was a light behind the curtain windows of the living room. From time to time, a shadow passed: Pofferi, then Jones. The rest of the house was in darkness. There was no action, but I waited until the light went out and a light went on in two of the bedrooms. I waited until those lights went out, then I climbed down and walked to the cottage.

While I watched, I had been using my brains. I decided that my first idea about going to Nancy, after she had been rescued and claiming that I had saved her, and how about some financial reward, was hasty thinking. I reminded myself that I had already tried to put the squeeze on her. She would be hostile when the time came for me to give her my respectful smile.

Bart, baby, I said to myself, you'll have to find a different approach. You need help to swing this. You need to give this a lot more thought.

I settled on the couch in the living room of the cottage, ate the beef sandwiches Jarvis had left me, and I worked at it until my brain began to creak. Around 02.15, I had a workable solution. I took a long look at this solution, decided it would hold together, patted myself on the back, then I went to sleep.

I woke as the sun came through the curtains. The time was 07.30. I roused myself, took a shower, shaved, dressed, then stepped out into the warm air, looking hopefully for Jarvis to bring breakfast.

When he did arrive, I was looking like an alert guard who had been on the job throughout the night.

I asked after the old nut.

"He is still very upset, Mr. Anderson," Jarvis said as he

164

placed the loaded tray on the table. "I am keeping him under sedation."

"Best thing," I said as I sat down. There were pancakes, sausages, grilled ham and a pile of scrambled eggs.

Jarvis sat by my side as I ate. He talked of his friend, Washington Smith. I listened and did a lot of sad head wagging, but the recital didn't stop me eating.

"It is something I can't understand," Jarvis said. "People who are rich enough to employ servants are unpredictable. To be dismissed after fifteen years service! It is quite shameful."

I said it was, finished the coffee, then patted his arm.

"I can't see that happening to you, Mr. Jarvis."

"I trust not, but Mr. Herschenheimer is also unpredictable."

Taking the tray, he left me. I went down to the tree, climbed it and surveyed the ranch house. Josh Jones was standing in the doorway of the front door, smoking. Around his waist, cowboy style, was a gun belt from which dangled a mean-looking .45. Hidden in the foliage of the tree, I watched him. He remained there, breathing in the warm air, motionless and menacing. I told myself that Coldwell and his men wouldn't have a picnic when they moved in.

After a while, he stepped back and closed the front door. I waited, but there was no further action. I wondered what was happening to Nancy. Maybe, like the old nut, she was under sedation.

When it was 11.30, I returned to the cottage and waited for Carl to relieve me. As soon as he arrived, I got in the Maser and headed for Mel Palmer's office.

Palmer's secretary was a sexy-looking doll with Venetian red hair and a bust line that would make a brigade of guards mis-step. She eyed me the way she would eye a roach in her soup.

"Mr. Palmer," I said, giving her my sexy smile. "Bart Anderson."

165

"Have you an appointment, Mr. Anderson?" Cool and distant as the moon.

"Just tell him. I don't need an appointment."

She hesitated, then rising from behind her desk, she went into an inner office. She was a tail-wagger: a condition that always makes me horny.

She stood in the doorway and jerked her head.

"Mr. Palmer will see you."

As I passed her, my right hand strayed, but that had happened to her countless times, and my hand encountered nothing.

Palmer, dwelling behind a big cigar, regarded me doubtfully.

"What is it, Anderson?"

I selected a comfortable chair and sat down.

"Your client, Mrs. Nancy Hamel," I said. "She is your client?"

"Of course. What about her?" He looked impatiently at his watch. "I have an important lunch date."

"This is something you will want to hear, and it can't be rushed. Did you know Mrs. Hamel had an identical twin sister?"

He blinked.

"No, but is that important?"

"The twin is Lucia Pofferi, an Italian terrorist wanted for two murders. Her husband, Aldo Pofferi, is also a terrorist; one of the leaders of the Italian Red Brigade, wanted for at least three murders, and I have proof he murdered Russ Hamel."

If I had driven a nail into his fat behind, he couldn't have reacted more. His face flushing, his eyes bulging, he jumped to his feet.

"Are you drunk?" he squealed. "How dare you say such a thing!"

"The FBI have the facts, and they are taking action tonight."

"Good God!" He sank into his chair and began mopping his face with a silk handkerchief.

166

"It's a complicated story," I said. "You had better hear it from the beginning. When it is finally sorted out, the publicity will be red hot. It can't do Hamel's books any harm. Handled right, it should treble his sales, and you're the man to handle it right."

That made him take notice as I knew it would. He put away his handkerchief and put on his business face.

I gave him the same story as I had given Lu Coldwell. I concluded by saying, "So the set-up is this: the two terrorists hold Nancy Hamel in her home. The woman who joined you when I found Hamel dead wasn't Nancy, but Lucia."

"Damn it! I'll swear it was Nancy," he muttered.

"Identical twins, and you saw her in half light and you were naturally shocked. Nancy will certainly be murdered once she has been forced to sign a batch of cheques which will give her sister access to Hamel's money."

He sat and thought, then he nodded.

"That would explain it. Only this morning, this woman telephoned me. She sounded hysterical. She told me she couldn't attend her husband's funeral and asked me to handle all the details. She asked me to leave her alone. She had to grieve by herself."

"Sure, that figures. Lucia wouldn't want to expose herself to a lot of mourners, and she's not risking seeing you again."

"Good God!" Palmer began to mop his face again.

"I'm going to make a suggestion to you, Mr. Palmer," I said, putting on my sincere expression. "I'm going to suggest that you appoint me as Mrs. Hamel's representative."

He stopped mopping his face and regarded me suspiciously.

"Mrs. Hamel's representative? What does that mean?"

"Someone, representing her, should be on the spot when the Pofferis are taken. Someone who can get Mrs. Hamel away before the press move in. Mrs. Hamel will be in shock. She must not be exposed to the press until she has

167

recovered." I leaned forward and stared hard at him. "You are Mrs. Hamel's representative. Do you want to be there during the gun battle? The FBI expect to kill both Pofferi and his wife. It will be a battlefield. Do you want to be there or do you want me to be there, acting on your behalf and Mrs. Hamel's behalf?"

He reacted as I knew he would react. The very thought of putting himself anywhere near a gun battle made his fat jowls quiver.

"Yes, yes, I see what you mean. Would you do that, Mr. Anderson?"

I put on my modest expression.

"That's my job. Leave this to me. I guarantee Mrs. Hamel's safety, and also guarantee the press won't get near her."

"How will you do that?" He frowned suspiciously. "How will you get her off the Largo without the press badgering her?"

I hadn't battered my brains for nothing. I had all the answers.

"By helicopter, Mr. Palmer. I have a good friend who owns a chopper. As soon as the battle is over, he will land on Hamel's lawn, and we'll whisk Mrs. Hamel away. I suggest you reserve a penthouse suite at the Spanish Bay hotel. They have a chopper landing pad on the roof. Mrs. Hamel can stay there until she recovers. The hotel won't let any unauthorised person near her."

His fat face brightened.

"That is an excellent idea. The Spanish Bay have a resident doctor and nurse should Mrs. Hamel need medical care. I'll leave the helicopter arrangement to you, Anderson. I will take care of the reservation. I must go now."

"There are two little things, Mr. Palmer," I said, giving him my boyish smile. "I need written authority from you that I am acting as Mrs. Hamel's representative. The FBI might be difficult unless they know I have official standing."

"Yes, yes." He called in his tail-wagging secretary and dictated to her the necessary authorization. "Get it typed right away."

She eyed me as she left the room.

"And the second thing?"

"Expenses. I'll need two thousand for the chopper and the pilot."

He stiffened.

"That's a lot of money."

"Danger money, Mr. Palmer. There's going to be a shoot-up. The money will come from Hamel's estate, so why should you care?"

"Yes, of course."

The secretary returned with the authorization, and Palmer signed it.

"Give Mr. Anderson two thousand dollars in cash, Miss Hills." Palmer shook my hand and made for the door. "When will this operation take place?"

"Tonight."

"I will be waiting at the hotel." Nodding, he was gone.

Miss Hills regarded me.

"Two thousand in cash?"

"That's what the man said."

I followed her out of the office, waited until she produced the money, then stowed the money in my wallet.

"Did anyone tell you you have big, beautiful eyes?" I said.

"Frequently," she returned coldly. "I'm busy. 'Bye, Mr. Anderson," and she sat down and began to type.

I filed her away for future reference. She would need working on. Now wasn't the time.

Bart, baby, I said to myself, as I climbed into the Maser, everything, so far, is going your way.

*   *   *

Zero hour was to be 03.00.

As Nancy Hamel's representative, plus the fact that I

169

had been inside the ranch house and knew its geography, I was given a seat at the round table in the conference room at the Mayor's office.

Mayor Hedley, Chief of Police Terrell, Sergeant Hess, together with Coldwell, Stoneham and Jackson of the FBI, were present.

Coldwell explained that the information he had revealed to the other men had come from an informer. No questions were asked about the informer. Coldwell went on to say that I was present as I had been instructed to get Mrs. Hamel away from the press as soon as the Pofferis had been taken.

I drew a plan of the ranch house, explained the electronic controls at the gate, explained that, as a guard working for Mr. Herschenheimer, I had been keeping watch on the ranch house and I knew where Nancy Hamel was located. I put an X on the map of the house.

After more talk, it was decided to cut off the electricity on the Largo so a silent entry could be made through the gates. Police guards were already in place. When the time came, the three FBI agents, supported by ten armed police would storm the house.

I then went on to tell them that I had arranged for Nick Hardy in his chopper to be overhead at Zero hour, and when Nancy Hamel was freed, I would be on the spot to convey her by air to the Spanish Bay hotel where Mel Palmer would be waiting to take care of her.

There were no objections, and the meeting broke up.

I had paid Nick Hardy five hundred dollars for his services. That left me fifteen hundred dollars in hand. The time when the meeting broke up was 19.30. I had a lot of hours to kill before the action. I returned to my apartment, hesitated, then called Bertha.

When she came on the line, I said, "Is that Mrs. Fink?" She giggled.

"Oh, you."

"Who else? Baby, I'm lonely. Are you married yet?"

"Next week, and listen, Bart, I told you we were

through. When I say a thing, I mean it!"

"Since when? Listen, baby, I have a wallet stuffed with the green. How about you and me sharing a gorgeous dinner at the Spanish Bay grill?"

"How did you get the money?" Bertha demanded.

"Don't ask silly questions. Do you or don't you want to share this meal with me?"

There was a long pause.

"I'm engaged to be married," she said feebly.

"Since when did that stop any right minded doll accepting an invitation?"

"Well, okay, Bart, but this will be the last time."

"Fine. We will eat at nine-thirty. Come over here right away, baby."

"If we are eating at nine-thirty, why should I come over to you right away?"

"Guess," I said, and hung up.

I drove Bertha back to her apartment around 01.30. It had been a very satisfactory evening. We had done our physical gymnastics together until it was time to eat. We had eaten a beautiful, sustaining meal, we had danced, then we had sat on the crowded terrace in the moonlight, holding hands.

"Bart, I wish this could go on forever," Bertha sighed. "I know you are a heel, but you are a beautiful heel."

I patted her hand.

"Get married, baby. Get some security. That's what really counts. Once you get it, you can enjoy yourself. Your fink won't know if you get something on the side. I'll be around." I gave her my boyish smile. "Next time, you'll pick up the check. Imagine! It will give you a marvellous lift."

She laughed.

"Bart! You're hopeless!"

Leaving her, I drove to Paradise Largo. There were two cops standing at the barrier with O'Flagherty. He came over to me, his eyes popping with excitement.

"This is going to be some night, Bart," he said.

"You can say that again."

The two cops came over and peered at me, then nodded to O'Flagherty who lifted the barrier.

It had been agreed at the meeting that Carl should be alerted. He opened the gates to let me in. He too was excited. We went up to the cottage to find Jarvis with drinks and sandwiches. I told them what was about to happen.

"There could be a lot of noise," I said. "Better give the old nut a real shot so he sleeps through it."

Jarvis said he had already done that.

I looked at my watch. Another hour. I ate the sandwiches, took a drink, then walked down to the tree.

So far, it was going beautifully, I thought, but the crunch would come when I walked in to take Nancy to the chopper. Man! Could that turn sour!

Suppose she recognized me and blew the whistle on me to Coldwell? I thought about this, and although the thought gave me goose pimples, I told myself in the heat of the moment, the noise, the confusion, the cops trampling around, she might not connect me with the guy who had tried to blackmail her. Besides, with luck she would be half doped. It was a gamble I had to take.

I climbed the tree. Immediately below me, I could see shadowy figures. The FBI and the cops were already gathering. I looked over at the ranch house. It was in total darkness.

I wondered if they had posted a guard: either Jones or Pofferi, but doubted it. They must have felt completely secure behind those electronically controlled gates and on the Largo.

I recognized Coldwell's tall figure.

"All in darkness," I called down softly. "No movement."

He glanced up, grunted, then drawing the group to him, he began going over his instructions again in a whisper.

The men were standing by the gates.

Faintly, in the distance, I could hear the approaching chopper. Nick had instructions from me to stay overhead until I flashed a torch, then he was to turn on his floods, and make a landing on Hamel's lawn.

Coldwell said, "The current's off."

The moon, coming from behind a dense pack of cloud, cast light on the gates.

I saw a car being pushed down the road by four cops. Coldwell and his men shoved open the gates and the four cops pushed the car onto the drive to the ranch house. They had some hundred of yards to cover before they reached the vast expanse of lawn. There they stopped. Coldwell's men fanned out and moved into the shrubs, keeping away from the nakedness of the lawn.

I was puzzled by the car until suddenly the headlights went on: not ordinary headlights, but powerful beams, specially fitted to the car.

The beams lit up the front of the house.

Coldwell, using a bull-horn, began yelling to Pofferi to come out with his hands in the air. His voice, greatly magnified, seemed to hit the house like the blows of a sledge hammer.

Nothing happened.

Coldwell's voice continued to hammer against the house. I felt a trickle of sweat run down my face.

Coldwell was taking no chances. He just kept yelling. All his men were now lying flat, concealed in the many flowering shrubs.

Still nothing happened.

Coldwell stopped yelling.

Overhead was the noisy clatter of the chopper, its lights winking. I wondered how Nick was enjoying this movie-like scene.

Then there came a clunk, and the first gas bomb smashed a window. A moment later, gas began to drift out onto the lawn.

Jones was the first to appear. He threw open the front door, then a gun blazing in his hand, he tried to run

173

towards the shadows, away from the blinding lights.

A gun banged and Jones reared back, clawing at the air. The gun banged again and Jones slid down on his knees and straightened out.

One down and two to go, I thought, watching tensely.

Coldwell began to bawl through the bull-horn.

"Pofferi! Come on out with your hands behind your head!"

The gas smoke was thinning. I thought of Nancy, and hoped they wouldn't fire more gas bombs.

Then out of the shadows at the far end of the house came gun fire. One of the headlights of the car went out. Flashes lit up the darkness. I heard a cop yell. Another cop sprang upright, then staggered back and dropped.

The other cops and the Agents directed a withering fire in the direction of the flashes. Then I saw Pofferi, outlined in the light of the single beam, a revolver in either hand, move crab-like, half bent double, his white shirt stained red with blood, but he kept firing.

A burst of gunfire. I saw bullets slam into him. He was swept off his feet and fell.

I wiped the sweat off my face.

Two down, and one to go.

"Come on out, Lucia!" Coldwell bawled. "With your hands behind your head!"

A long pause, then I heard screams. Lucia came out into the dazzling light as if she had been projected from a cannon.

I saw her clearly.

She had on black slacks and a scarlet shirt. As she staggered through the doorway, she screamed, "Don't shoot!" Her hands were waving frantically. She had an object in each hand. She hadn't taken more than ten steps before she exploded.

There were two blinding flashes, two bangs that sent me rocking on the tree branch, then the whistling sound of shrapnel.

Rather than be taken, Lucia had blown herself to

174

pieces, Japanese style, with hand grenades.

I looked down at the scene, feeling sick. All that was left of Lucia Pofferi was a ghastly mess of ripped flesh, intestines and shattered bones.

It was the finish!

I shinned down the tree, ran across the road, paused to signal to Nick, hovering overhead, then ran up the drive.

The Agents and the cops were moving around: some of them attending to the two wounded cops, some checking Jones' body, others Pofferi's body. Coldwell was staring at the gruesome remains of Lucia.

I didn't stop. I ran into the house, ran down the long corridor, pausing to throw open doors until I reached a locked door.

The gas smoke was now so weak, it only irritated my eyes. Standing back, I slammed my foot against the lock of the door. As I did so the electric current was restored and the corridor lit up.

The door swung open.

I stood in the open doorway, looking into a big, lighted room: a woman's luxury bedroom. There was a double bed facing me. Sitting on the bed, her face in her hands, was Nancy Hamel. She was shivering, and frightened whimpers came from her.

Bart, baby, I thought, if she recognizes you and flips her lid, this set-up is going to turn sour. I moved slowly into the room.

"Mrs. Hamel."

She stiffened, snatched her hands from her face and stared at me. Her eyes were wide, her mouth slack. Then like a frightened animal, she sprang to her feet.

"It's all right, Mrs. Hamel," I said in my soothing voice. "You are safe."

She stared at me.

"My sister!" Her hands covered her face and she moaned. "She said she would kill herself. What happened?"

I began to relax. She hadn't recognized me!

"It's over, Mrs. Hamel," I said. "I'm here to take you away from all this. Mr. Palmer has arranged to get you to the Spanish Bay hotel where you can rest. There's a helicopter waiting."

"Lucia is dead?" She stared at me. "They are all dead?"

"Yes. Let's go, Mrs. Hamel. Is there anything you want to take with you?"

She hid her face and began to sob.

I waited, looking at her. She was wearing a dark green trouser suit. If she was to stay out of sight at the Spanish Bay hotel, she would need other clothes. I looked helplessly around.

"Mrs. Hamel!" I put a bark in my voice. 'You'll need things. Let me help you pack."

She shuddered, then waved to a closet.

"The bag."

I opened the closet door and found a big suitcase.

"Lucia told me to pack," Nancy said. "She knew this was the end."

"Let's go." I lifted the suitcase as Coldwell came to the door. "All set, Lu," I said. "Take the bag. I'll help Mrs. Hamel."

I went to her and pulled her gently to her feet. With my arm around her, I led her to the front door. The car lights had been turned off, but the smell of Lucia's disintegrated body hung foully on the hot air.

Nancy took one breath, screamed and fainted. I just managed to catch her, then scooping her up in my arms, hurried across to the waiting chopper. Coldwell helped me lift her inert body into the chopper.

Nick, his eyes bugging, took her from us and laid her across the back seat. Coldwell pushed in the suitcase, then stood back.

"Let's go," I said as I dropped into the seat beside Nick.

"Man! I saw it all!" he exclaimed as he gunned the engine. "I wouldn't have missed it for the world!"

I wasn't listening. As the chopper lifted, I turned

around to look at Nancy. Her face was white, her eyes closed.

So far, fine, I thought. She hasn't recognized me, but she surely must when she is out of shock. Play one card at the time. At least, you have established the fact that it was you who rescued her.

It took less than ten minutes for Nick to land on the Spanish Bay hotel helicopter pad. As he switched on the landing lights, I could see Mel Palmer, a nurse and two white coated interns, waiting.

As the chopper grounded, Nancy stirred, then sat up.

"What's happening?" she demanded shrilly. "Where am I?"

I turned to face her. The light in the cabin was strong enough to light both our faces.

"Mrs. Hamel, you are safe," I said. "You're at the Spanish Bay hotel and Mr. Palmer is waiting to take care of you."

She stared fixedly at me.

"Who are you?"

"The guy who rescued you," I said, and gave her my boyish smile, but I was puzzled. It was hard to accept that she didn't remember that time when we had sat facing each other on the terrace of the Country Club when I had tried to put the squeeze on her, but I could see she didn't remember, and I began to relax. "You have nothing to worry about. You are now safe."

Nick opened the door of the chopper. I slid out. Nancy got unsteadily to her feet. Nick helped her descend and I took over. She leaned against me as Palmer came fussily up.

The two interns took over. I stepped back to give Palmer room to go into his soothing act.

For tonight, there was nothing more I could do. I watched her being led across the roof with Palmer murmuring. Then at the elevator that would take them down to the penthouse, she abruptly turned.

"Where's my bag?"

177

The strident, urgent snap in her voice was a complete give away. Up to this moment, she had had me fooled, but that snap in her voice sent a cold prickle up my spine. That wasn't the voice of a woman who had just lost her sister, just lost her husband, a woman everyone described as "nice". This was the voice of a dangerous, ruthless terrorist!

For a long moment, I stood still, absorbing the shock. Then my brain moved into action. Here was the answer to the puzzle why this woman I had thought was Nancy hadn't recognized me. *Lucia Pofferi had never seen me! So how could she recognize me?* Into my mind flashed the picture of the woman I had thought was Lucia, staggering out of the ranch house, screaming: *Don't shoot!* Lucia had sacrificed her sister in a ruthless attempt to escape! She had strapped live grenades to Nancy's hands, then kicked her out into the open, knowing when the grenades exploded, her sister's body would be a mess of broken bones and flesh, obliterating her hands and her finger prints.

But this gruesome escape plan had come apart at the seams. Lucia had made two fatal errors: she had failed to recognize me because she had never seen me, and the suitcase she had packed was so important to her, she had let her mask slip.

I forced myself to call, "It's all right, Mrs. Hamel. I'm bringing it."

The two interns closed around her. They and Palmer entered the elevator cage with her.

Nick handed down the suitcase.

"That's it, Nick, and thanks. Don't say a word to the press."

"It's been a ball," Nick said, grinning. "Man! This is something to tell my grandchildren."

I crossed over to the elevator, paused until he had taken off, then tried to open the suitcase. It was locked. Using the barrel of my gun, I forced open the locks.

Among the clothes, I found a .38 revolver, two hand grenades and a cheque book. Squatting on my haunches, I examined the cheque book. Every cheque in the book carried Nancy Hamel's signature. Staring at the book, I realized the book was worth millions of dollars. I put it in my jacket pocket, then I hid the revolver and the grenades in the gutter, surrounding the roof. I carefully re-fixed the locks, then I took the elevator down to the penthouse floor. I found Mel Palmer, looking miffed, standing outside a door in the corridor.

"Mr. Anderson," he said. "She wants her bag."

"I bet she does," I said.

"I don't understand it" he went on, a plaintive whine in his voice. "She refuses medical care. She said she wanted to be alone. After all the trouble I have taken to arrange for her comfort! She actually pushed me out!"

That I could understand.

"I'll give her the bag," I said. "She has had a great shock. The best thing for her is to get some rest."

"It's nearly dawn!" he exclaimed. "I also need rest! I have commitments today! I am going home."

"The best place, Mr. Palmer," I said, giving him my sincere smile. "As soon as I have given Mrs. Hamel her bag, that's where I'll be heading."

I watched him walk to the elevator, then I loosened my gun in its holster, then tapped on the door.

"Your bag, Mrs. Hamel," I said.

The door jerked open.

The woman I was now sure was Lucia Pofferi stared at me. Her face had a boney, scraped look: her eyes were glittering.

"Put it down," she said, taking a step back.

I moved forward and placed the bag just inside the room.

"Thank you," she said. "Now leave me."

With the heel of my shoe, I shoved the door shut. As I did so, I drew my gun and levelled it at her.

"Take it easy, baby," I said. "Don't try anything tricky."

She cocked an eyebrow.

"So, who are you?"

"The name's Bart Anderson."

Watching her, I saw her eyes narrow. The nickel had dropped. Diaz must have told her my name: possibly Nancy also.

"Bart Anderson?" A thin, viperish smile touched her lips.

"Of course, the blackmailer. How did you get on the scene?"

"It's my business. Let's sit down, baby, we have much to talk about."

She shrugged, then walked over to a big settee and sat down. She crossed her legs and leaned back, regarding me. She looked as attractive as a coiled cobra. I took a chair well away from her and I kept the gun pointing at her.

"How does it feel to murder your sister?" I asked

"That ninny? Why not? She was a useless bird-brain. Aldo agreed she should take my place. I am important to our movement. She was nothing." Her eyes moved to the suitcase. "I see you've broken the locks. Did you get the cheque book?"

"I have it." I smiled at her. "The hardware is up on the roof."

She nodded.

"So let's not waste time," she said. "How much do you want?"

Still keeping her covered, I took out the cheque book and waved it at her.

"I'll settle for a million. That leaves you plenty. Let's work it this way: I keep the cheques. You stay here. I'll write four cheques for two hundred and fifty thousand. When the loot has been transferred to my bank, I'll give you the book. It'll take a week or so. Then I'll help you get away. There's the yacht, baby. I'll find a crewman and one dark night, you take off for Cuba. Like the idea?"

Her face remained a stony mask.

"Yes, I like it," she said finally, "but suppose after you have had your pay-off, you drop out of sight?"

"There's that," I said, giving her my boyish smile. "I guess you'll have to trust me."

She shook her head.

"I have a better idea. Take four of those cheques and give me the rest. I'll stay here a week to give you time to get your share, then I'll start cashing my cheques. Anything wrong in that?"

I once again began to dream of owning a million dollars, and when I begin to dream about money, I lose concentration.

"Fine with me," I said, and did a fatal thing. I was sitting well away from her, so I put my gun on the arm of my chair and began to count out four cheques. While doing this, I took my eyes off her: another fatal mistake. Then as she moved, I dropped the cheque book and grabbed for my gun, but I was much too late.

She had a gun in her hand and was shooting before my fingers touched my gun. She must have had the gun hidden down the side of the settee.

I felt a thud against my chest, then saw the gun flash, then heard the bang, and that's all I did see and hear.

My million dollar world exploded into darkness.

*   *   *

I wasn't allowed to see any visitors for a week. I lay in a hospital bed, feeling sorry for myself and being attended to by a middle-aged nurse who was as sexy as a dead star fish. From time to time, the surgeon would come in and congratulate himself on saving my life. He had a laugh like a hyena: he looked like a hyena.

While I lay in bed, I did some thinking. It looked as if I was back on square A, and once I was up and about again, I would have to begin my dreary life, working for the Agency. I asked the nurse what had happened. She said she didn't know: just looking at her, I wasn't surprised. She was the type who worked in her small circle and let the world go by. So I just lay there and wondered until my first visitor arrived: Lu Coldwell.

As he drew up a chair and sat down, he said, "You had a lucky escape, Bart. What happened?"

"I gave her her suitcase," I said. "Then as I was leaving, she pulled a gun and shot me."

- "What the hell did she do that for?"

"You ask her. Don't ask me."

"The shot was heard. The hotel dick went up to investigate, and she shot him. Then she took the elevator down to the lobby and walked out, carrying the suitcase and the gun in her hand. You can imagine the commotion! A patrol car was passing, spotted her, carrying a gun, pulled up and she started shooting. They cut her down. She was dead on arrival."

"She must have gone berserk," I said.

"She was Lucia Pofferi. Nancy Hamel died at the ranch house."

So it is over, I thought. No million, back to the treadmill.

"The way I figure it is this . . ." Coldwell said, and went on to tell me what I could have told him. I didn't bother to listen.

When he was through, the nurse came in and said I should rest. Coldwell said he hoped I'd be around again soon and took himself off.

No one came near me for the next week. I led a lonely life. I hoped Bertha might at least send flowers: nothing from her. She was now probably married to her Fink and cruising somewhere in his yacht.

I was sitting up in a chair by the time I had my second visitor. It was Chick Barley. He came in, carrying a bottle of Cutty Sark.

"Hi, Bart! How are they hanging?"

I dredged up a brave smile and accepted the bottle.

"I'm making progress," I said. "Good of you to come. No one else has bothered."

"Yeah." He began to wander around the room, and I could see he had something on his mind.

"Any news of Bertha?" I asked, hopefully.

"She got married. She's gone off to Europe for the honeymoon. The guy she married is loaded with the green."

I felt even more depressed. I watched Chick move around the room, hands in his pockets, a frown on his face. I felt sure he was full of bad news.

"What's biting you, Chick?" I said. "Something on your mind?"

"Robertson's Law Index," he said, pausing in his prowling. "You have a copy . . . right?"

I gaped at him.

"Yeah. God knows why I bought it. I've never looked at it."

"The Colonel left his copy at home, and started yelling for one. I remembered you had a copy, so I dug it out of your Scotch drawer and gave it to him."

"Okay, so you gave it to him. So what?"

Then my heart gave a bound and I felt cold. I remembered I had put a copy of my blackmailing statement about Pofferi, the pirates' island and the Alameda which I had hoped would screw a hundred thousand dollars out of Nancy Hamel in that book. The statement hadn't been in an envelope! The Colonel would have read it! The Colonel was nobody's fool. He would know I had been on the scene at the beginning, and why.

I saw Chick was regarding me.

"I'm sorry," he said. "How was I to know? Glenda told me to tell you. Jesus, Bart! How could you have done such a goddamn thing?"

"Yeah." Cold sweat was running down my back. "So I am a dope. It looked good, Chick."

He grimaced.

"Blackmail never looks good. Now, listen, the Colonel isn't taking police action. He told Glenda if he did, the stink would smear the Agency's image."

I began to brighten.

"The Colonel's smart."

"Yeah, he's smart, but Bart, he's cancelled your licence, and he has put out the word. No one's going to touch you. I'm sorry, but that's the way it is." He stuck out his hand. "So long, Bart, and the best of luck."

When he had gone, I sat staring out of the window, down at the busy Paradise Avenue. I felt scared. Without a licence, I would now be way out on the unemployment limb.

Man! Was I depressed!

Later, the surgeon came in, grinning like a hyena. He said I could go home in a couple of days. I would have to take it easy, but in a month, I would be as good as new.

That I knew I wouldn't be. Left alone, my mind was like a frightened squirrel in a cage. I had about two thousand dollars between me and the bread-line. I had the hospital charges to meet. I would have to hunt for a job.

I stewed for two days and two nights, scarcely sleeping. I found no solution as to how I could earn the money I needed to live up to my standards.

Chick, my loyal pal, had sent over a suitcase of my clothes from my apartment, and he had parked the Maser outside the hospital. He also enclosed an envelope containing a fifty dollar bill with a note: *For the last time. I'll miss financing you, old pal.*

I drove back to my apartment, feeling lower than a snake's belly. I opened the front door, then paused. The big living room looked like a florist's shop: flowers everywhere. There was a small banner stretched across the over-mantel that read: WELCOME BACK HOME, YOU HEEL.

I crossed the room and threw open my bedroom door. There was Bertha, naked as the back of my hand, lying seductively on my bed.

"You were shot, huh?" she said.

Was I glad to see her!

"I was shot." I closed the door.

"Where?"

I grinned at her.

"Not where you think," and I began to toss off my clothes.

Twenty minutes later, we lay side by side. Bertha kept running her fingers through my hair, making soft moaning noises. If that was her after-play, I went along with it, but already my mind was nibbling at my future.

"Bart, darling," she said. "I am now sure I can't go along with Theo."

I patted her bare bottom.

"Theo?"

"My husband."

"For God's sake! Is that his name?"

"Theo Danrimpel: the Fink with the millions."

I sat up.

"You mean you married *that* guy! He's as rich as Ford!"

She pushed me back, leaned over me and began to nibble my ear.

"I married him, honey, but you can't imagine! I know you are a heel, but what a lovely heel! I need you. I can't live with a fink who just sits and watches. A girl must have her own, intimate life."

"That I can understand, but how would I fit in?"

"How would you like to live in Palm Springs, honey? Theo has a big estate. There is a gorgeous little cottage for you. Theo knows I need a boy friend. He's marvellously understanding. How about it?"

Suddenly the clouds lifted, the sky was blue again and the sun shone.

As a status symbol, a gigolo was way ahead of a blackmailer.

Me, Bertha and Theo were about to begin a beautiful, lush-plush partnership.

If I played my cards right (and Man! I was certainly going to play them right!) I was now not going to starve.

The End

>>> If you've enjoyed this book and would like to discover more great vintage crime and thriller titles, as well as the most exciting crime and thriller authors writing today, visit: >>>

The Murder Room
Where Criminal Minds Meet

themurderroom.com